Once Again

Once Again

A Novel

CATHERINE WALLACE HOPE

alcove
press

Published in the United States by Alcove Press, an imprint of The Quick Brown Fox & Company LLC.

Alcove Press and its logo are trademarks of The Quick Brown Fox & Company LLC.

Library of Congress Catalog-in-Publication data available upon request.

ISBN (hardcover): 978-1-64385-481-6
ISBN (ebook): 978-1-64385-482-3

Cover design by Melanie Sun

Printed in the United States.

www.alcovepress.com

Alcove Press
34 West 27th St., 10th Floor
New York, NY 10001

First Edition: October 2020

10 9 8 7 6 5 4 3 2 1

For Peter, Tim, Neill, and George

Demeter, the harvest goddess, and Zeus, the sky god, had a daughter, Persephone—a girl as delicate as the flowers she loved to pick. One day, tempted by wondrous narcissus blooms, she wandered away on her own. Suddenly, the earth opened beneath her, and Hades, the king of the underworld, lunged upward out of the ground in his chariot driven by four immortal black horses. He seized her against her will and dragged her down into the abyss and made her his queen.

Demeter knew nothing of what had happened. Her grief at the loss of her child was so deep that she allowed no crops to grow, and the world starved. She neither ate nor drank, but traveled over land and sea, searching for the truth. When at last she learned of the abduction, she approached the gates of hell and demanded her daughter's return. But before he conceded, Hades sat on a funeral couch with his three-headed hellhound at his feet. He drew his bride close and tricked her into eating a few seeds of pomegranate to make their bond indissoluble so he could keep her, at least for a portion of each year, in his dark realm. And so it was that she could never escape the land of the dead during the season of winter's bitter sleep.

—Drawn from the *Homeric Hymns*, anonymous

PART I

The Ring

Chapter One

9:20 AM
Sunday, June 20, 2021 | The 500th day | 371 Nysa Vale
Road, Boulder, Colorado

Erin Fullarton sat at the island in her kitchen, alone. Wearing the T-shirt and sweatpants from the day before, or maybe the day before that, she shivered slightly, even though the room felt warm. She cradled a cup in her hands, but the remnants of her coffee were cold. *Once there was a ghost,* she thought. This was the game she and her daughter used to play, telling each other little stories they made up together, five words a turn.

Erin closed her eyes and let herself see Korrie's face, those round, lucent gray eyes, the way she used to gaze to the side as she searched for words. In the beginning, when Korrie was three and just beginning to figure out the game, she ended every story with her main character—a fairy, a hamster, a fish—successfully going potty, which she found hilarious. She had that little-girl laugh that tumbled across the room as loud as a chord on a harmonica. By the time she was six, shortly before her death, the stories had become more sophisticated, with missions to rescue captured sisters and find lost undersea homelands.

Now, Erin took Korrie's turn and filled in the words for her "*. . . who lived in the woods.*" Erin put her cup down on the white countertop of the island. "Stop it," she muttered. "Stop turning it into a story for her." But she couldn't make herself stop. It had been nearly a year and a half since Korrie died—five hundred days—and still, all Erin could do was think of her. She couldn't start new things. She couldn't make lists. She couldn't reach out to other people. She couldn't find her way back to the normal world. *Because,* she thought, *this is what becomes of the mother of a murdered child.*

She would never have guessed there would come a time in her marriage when she could no longer talk to Zac about Korrie. But it was true; she just couldn't. And she couldn't stand by and witness his struggle. He still tried so hard to be a good father to Korrie, even now. He posted remembrances. He donated picture books to the library in her name. He tended her grave.

It was too painful for Erin to be around him all the time. Despite everything, he seemed to be still alive inside. Stricken, but living. Able to work, able to function in a basic, practical sense. She couldn't bear to see him day in and day out, wearing his sorrow like a wool sweater, forcing himself to carry on with the meaningless trivialities of day-to-day life, trying to be the husband she needed. She didn't welcome his attempts to console her, and she wouldn't listen to anything he had to say. So he'd agreed to live away from her for a while. For the last few months, he'd been staying at his brother's house. Dan and his fiancée, Maggie, lived nearby in Nederland, and they, too, were hovering in a holding pattern. Because how could anyone continue with their plans now?

But Erin would try her hardest to make a plan for this day. The therapist who ran her Grief Group suggested a time line on which she could mark her progress. "Make it round numbers if you want," Dr. Tanner had said. "As neutral as simple addition, so there's no emotional charge. Just days adding up to a milestone."

Five hundred. My God.

"Imagine them adding up to a turning point in the future," he'd said. But how? That was the question. How could there be a turning point when all the days that gathered on the floor at her feet were so much like the ones before?

She took her phone from the pocket of her sweatpants and checked to see if it was still too early or if it was time to call Zac yet. 9:20. June 20, 2021. A symbol for clear skies, and a current temperature of seventy-eight degrees. She decided to wait until 9:30 to call, stick to the schedule. Zac had been checking on her several times a day, until she'd asked him to stop. It had made her feel like his patient, so they'd agreed on a schedule. In the mornings, she called him at the designated time, and they said their designated things, and that was it for the day. This was the last pattern left in her life: coffee, call Zac, creep through the hours until the dark comes back, sleep until the dark splits open and the light crashes in.

To fill the sliver of time, she got up, took her pen and notebook from the counter, and sat again at the island. As she flipped open the notebook, light fell across her engagement ring. It had slipped to the knuckle of her third finger. She'd lost weight, and the ring was too loose now. Zac had already dropped off her wedding band at the jeweler's to be sized, but she wouldn't let him leave her engagement ring with a stranger. She slid it back into place and tipped her hand in the light so the sharp little diamond would scatter flecks of spectra across the granite.

When they were still back at Berkeley, Zac had had the ring made and then kept it hidden from her. One night, he asked if she would like to go out for dinner, telling her he had fulfilled a major step toward his astrophysics dissertation and he wanted to celebrate. At the time, she wondered if he would remember it was also the anniversary of the day they'd moved in together.

Zac kept their destination a surprise, refusing to tell her anything even as he parked at the curb, gave his keys to an attendant, and led her to the entrance of a building marked only by a number. To the right of the doorway, an intercom shone blue at eye level. Zac pushed the button. When a voice responded, he said, "Fullarton, party of two." He smiled, guilty and happy, like someone caught wrapping a present.

"What is going *on*?" Erin said, relishing the fun of his ruse.

"Nothing special." He laughed out loud then, sounding so pleased with himself.

A young man in a black cotton uniform appeared and opened the door for them. The air inside smelled of something savory and of rosemary, maple, and wine.

"Oh," Erin said, "I know where we are!" She'd heard of the secret restaurant and the fortune it cost to experience it. She squeezed Zac's hand. "Are you out of your mind?"

"Yeah, probably." He pulled her into a quick hug.

They followed the waiter through the deep, dim dining room, where scattered tables were lit like pieces of art.

"You are unbelievable," Erin whispered as they wended back toward the far end of the building.

"I know." Zac laughed again and squeezed her hand in return.

The waiter seated them at a table beside floor-to-ceiling glass that allowed a view of the activity within the kitchen.

"Zac," Erin said once they were alone, "you wouldn't believe how much I've wanted to come to this place. And sit at *this* table."

"I thought you'd like it," he said, and he stroked the back of her hand.

As the waitstaff circulated like bees, Erin turned and watched the performance of the chef and his staff. It was such an insider's pleasure to watch the choreography. She and Zac joked about what the kitchen crew might really be saying as they twirled knives, tossed skillets, and whacked filets in half.

The aroma coming from the table's centerpiece changed to citrus as the waiter poured a concoction over it and then served the first course. Black truffle and parmesan in a pressed apple cone—a miniature sculpture on an enormous plate. After the waiter left them, Zac studied the dish for a second and said, "We're going to need smaller forks."

A new glass of wine introduced another course, lobster in butter and ginger, followed by wagyu beef, morel, and sherry. "This is exactly how I'd do this," Erin said. "It's so perfect." She could almost see her future self in a crisp chef's jacket, creating something ephemeral but extraordinary that people would remember for their entire lives. It was an impractical choice—Berkeley's culinary school—and it was definitely not the path her family wanted her to take, but it was what she loved. Even when she was younger and all she could cook by herself was a grilled cheese sandwich, she'd made it special by trimming it into a heart shape with a cookie cutter and accenting it with an apple-peel rose.

Zac said, "I'm a willing victim if you ever want to try this at home."

"I might—you never know," she said with a smile, "but I'd need a set of teeny tiny cookware."

The two of them laughed over otoro tuna with salted plum and pink cherries, squab and brie and pears—one course after another for hours while the rest of the world seemed to blur away.

Once the pâtissier had cracked open their chocolate desserts, Erin said, "So, now, tell me what the news is for your dissertation. What step did you finish that deserves this much celebration?"

"Well," Zac paused. He smiled and tugged at his shirt. "I have a question for you, actually."

"Sure," she said. "What?"

"More of a statement, I guess." He reached into his pocket and pulled out a small, black-velvet ring box. "I'd really love it," he said, "if we got married."

A warm euphoria splashed over her, and she leaned closer to him, his handsome face waiting for her answer, his eyes locked on hers. They'd already talked vaguely about engagement, officializing their happy entanglement, but now it was truly the moment, and Erin's heart felt ticklish with joy. "I'd really love that too," she said, and she kissed his sweet lips, tasting of melted chocolate.

"Then this is for you," he said. He opened the box and showed her a ring, its small, sparkling diamond set in a simple gold band. As he slid the ring onto her third finger, the moment didn't feel like the adult event she would have imagined, but more like two youngsters plotting a trip into the wild.

The gemstone displayed its fire, even in the sparse lighting. "Wow, Zac," she said. "This is absolutely beautiful." She tilted her hand in the light so Zac could see the sparkle too.

"It's the only one of its kind."

She noted the stone's unusual shape, sharp and sitting up high off the band. "Because of the way it's set?"

"Because it's a clock." He grinned. "The dissertation thing. This is the time crystal."

"Are you kidding?" It was something he'd talked about since they'd first met. "I thought that was impossible," Erin said. "Or just theoretical."

"It was," he said, beaming, "until this."

She looked into his eyes, reveled in their connection for an instant, and then shook her head. She knew his accomplishment was something quite remarkable and that the scientific community would take notice. "I need you to explain it to me, how it can be a clock."

"Well," he said, "let me—well, feel free to stop me if I start droning on."

"I will," she said.

"The atoms in diamonds form a lattice. They're like a million microscopic magnets in a pattern in the three dimensions of space, right?"

His face took on the boyishness of fascination, and Erin loved his excitement. "Right," she said.

He told her about his special technique—using laser blasts to throw the electrons in the diamond's atoms out of equilibrium. He said they would continually shift positions to try to self-correct. "But by this time," he said, "they've forgotten where they started, so they fall into a state of cryptoequilibrium, endlessly oscillating, like a clock ticking forever, as they search for something that can never actually be found."

"Amazing." Erin could almost grasp the idea. "And they're doing that right now?" she said. "The electrons?"

"Yep, with absolute precision." Zac took her fingers in his. "In the heart of this chamber, beating for eons like a nanoscale clock." He tilted the stone toward the light.

"Another cool thing," he said, "sort of an elegant side effect, is that when the electron adjacent to the flaw got excited, the two locations formed a bond that emits luminescence. You can't actually see it with the naked eye, but now that it's in a time crystal, the luminescence can kind of slip between layers of time like a ghost." He let go of her hand.

She peered keenly into the stone. "You can give this to me?"

A waiter crowded in beside her and refilled her water glass. Her instinct was to protect the ring with her other hand.

Once the waiter was gone, Zac said, "I can."

"Are you sure it doesn't belong in the Smithsonian or somewhere?"

"Maybe." He widened his eyes a bit. "But after I submitted the paper, I bought the diamond from the lab. It belongs to me. And I can give it to you, now that we're into this whole marriage idea."

That beautiful spring night in the secret restaurant seemed like a thousand years ago. Though Erin had not been apart from the ring in all the time since then, here she was now, without Zac.

She drew in a breath and pulled her mind from the snare of ruminating about the past. She had to make something of this day. There had to be a remembrance to mark it. She and Zac should acknowledge it together, as Korrie's parents. Maybe she could bake muffins for later. Zac could come home for a little while, and they'd split and butter the muffins the way they used to, and have hot coffee, and it would make him glad to see she'd been able to accomplish something.

She forced herself to stand and cross to the old gas range. She turned the knob to "Bake" and set the temperature, but the oven didn't make its usual sound of ignition. The pilot light, out again. She found a box of matches, the only one left of the ones she'd ordered the winter Korrie died, with the Christmas photo of the three of them on the front. She opened the oven, relit the pilot, and slipped the matches in her pocket, this last box of the special ones. She turned to the cupboard. Maybe today could be that turning point her therapist prescribed. She found a muffin tin, muffin cups, pulled down flour, salt, baking powder, honey, and vanilla, and from the fridge she lugged butter, cream, and eggs.

From a shelf below, she got two bowls. A spoon. She needed a wooden spoon. And a whisk. Did she even know where the whisk was anymore? And with that, she was overwhelmed and could not face it. She turned the oven off. There had been a time when she could have put muffins together without a thought, frosted the cooled tops with buttercream like an artist with paints, but now she couldn't handle the idea of even starting them.

She turned toward the oncoming light of the day and peered out through the kitchen window. Beyond the glass, the arms of a blue spruce tree swept lightly north and then relaxed and fell back into place. Their two-story, two-bedroom stone cottage sat on ten wooded acres of mountain terrain above Boulder, their access road winding through a grove of tall blue spruces. It had been eighteen months since the closest of those trees was decorated as high as she and Zac and Korrie could reach, with homemade ornaments and fairy lights and winterberry chains. Now, summer sun poked through the highest branches in flickering pinpricks, and she tried to remember where those decorations had ended up. In Korrie's room? No, not there. So where then? How could it be that she didn't know?

She abandoned the idea of baking muffins and returned to her notebook. On a fresh page, in her spidery calligraphy, she wrote: *Sunday, June 20, 2021. Day 500.* She was supposed to let what was trapped inside escape onto these pages. Prove to herself that she was making an effort. After a pause, she skipped down two lines. *Same,* she wrote. Nothing there for Group to peck at, though they would certainly make the attempt. The ten of them would meet with Dr. Tanner in his tranquil office tomorrow morning, perched on pillowy chairs, sipping chamomile tea from cups decorated with honeybees and dragonflies.

I should skip Group if I don't have anything to share. That was the excuse she gave herself, but in reality, Group had devolved into a competition, with some of the mothers vying for the spot as top patient, determined to show how progress was made, each one willing to share her most earnest notes to show how *her* loss was the most profound, because none of the others knew *her* child. No one could know what it was to lose *that* child. And thus, her progress was the most hard fought; hers, the effort Dr. Tanner would most admire. And all of that was understandable. Yet lately, a sense of hierarchy had formed, an atmosphere of judgment about those who were trying to move forward versus those who refused.

One reason Erin had originally agreed to go was that she wanted someone to reassure her that she'd been a good mother, before. And that it hadn't all been swept away by what had happened. But it wasn't that kind of group.

On the page in front of her, she underlined the numerals three times and crossed out the word she'd written. What could she tell those women? Dr. Tanner? Tell them once again how a couple of trivial mistakes had cost her everything? How no penance could bring Korrie back? And how the threads that bound Erin to this world now were so thin, spun glass finer than spider silk. So easily snipped between her fingernails. She could sever them in a heartbeat.

One ordinary day in the last springtime of Korrie's life, Erin had taken her for a hike up a gentle trail through the hills, to gather wildflowers for the house. The two of them hiked a shady slope through the aspen. Korrie skipped ahead in her flouncy summer outfit, her dark curls bouncing against her back, hands bobbing as she conducted the music of her own made-up tune. She hopped over fallen branches, stopped, and galloped back.

Beside the trail, a small brook wove idly downhill. Sunlight broke through the canopy in dusty slants and glinted on the surface, and water striders rowed around on the mirror of a slow eddy. Erin edged closer to the brook and inhaled the sweet grassy fragrance. Korrie joined her, and Erin followed the direction of her gaze as she watched small alpine butterflies, moss elfins and hairstreaks and lupine blues, dropping down to the flattest stones to approach the rim of the water.

Korrie's expression transformed with wonderment. "Look!" she whispered. "See all the butterflies?" She turned her head toward the origin of the brook and then the other way, all along its curves. A smile of discovery lit her face. "This," she said, and she extended her arms parallel to the flow of the water, "this is the place where butterflies come to drink," as if it were the one magical spot in the whole world that they all returned to.

No. Erin wouldn't share that with Group. She would give them nothing. But tomorrow she would get dressed and force herself to show up because she'd promised Zac she would.

At 9:30, she pressed her phone awake and touched a square to access "Favorites." Of all the faces who had previously resided there, now only one remained. In his small circle, Zac smiled. She knew important things were happening at his job, but she needed him to set aside time today for this milestone if it was going to mean anything. Her request of him would be simple, brief. She would ask him to come home just for a little while, so she wouldn't be alone in the motionless ether, and to stay long enough to acknowledge this five-hundredth day since Korrie's death.

Erin tried to remember what she had been like with Zac before, who she'd once been, how she'd sounded, and she wondered if she could sound like that person again.

"It's time," she said. She pressed the image of his face and drew the phone up to her ear to listen for the sound of his voice.

Chapter Two

~

9:30 AM
Sunday, June 20, 2021 | National Institute of Standards and
Technology, Boulder, Colorado

Zac stepped into his office, flipped on the lights, and closed the door behind him. With a deep inhale, he tried to ease the constriction in his chest. The hour had almost arrived, and he didn't feel ready. His eyes ached, his cheeks were shaggy with stubble, and his mind was racing in a state of accelerated vigilance. He'd done all he could do this morning to prepare, to set things up before the others arrived. The guys on his team were his best friends, and he knew their habits. Mark would be on time, no matter how late they'd worked the night before; Jin would be late because he was always late; and Walter, with his supervisory prerogative, would breeze in whenever it suited him. Zac had gone to the other building, opened the Clean Room, and verified the thermal shield of the new atomic clock. Today's endeavor had officially begun when he switched it to "On Duty." With the spectroscope, he confirmed the frequency of the clock's new time crystal, only the second one in the world that could keep time in perpetuity without a supporting pacemaker of lasers. He calibrated the spectroscope, measuring the crystal's pulse to account for the electromagnetic field it generated and the pattern it created with the energy field broadcast by his own heartbeat.

These were the steps he'd taken to begin this momentous day, and then he had come back here to his office, to stick to his ordinary schedule, here behind the privacy of a closed door so he could take his call from Erin.

The other Erin, as he'd begun thinking of her, the one who'd replaced his wife, this lifeless Erinesque version who had appeared when the love of his life, mother of his child, was sucked into the void. When Korrie died, Erin departed without him for regions unknown. First Korrie and then Erin.

She called at 9:30, the appointed time. He could hear in her voice that she was trying to sound upbeat, but a chill lay beneath the words. "I would have called you before you left for work, but I—" She paused. "I don't know."

He didn't tell her he'd stopped staying with Dan and Maggie. Whenever he saw them, they tried to take care of him, and that made him feel as crushable as a naked hatchling caught out of its shell. So for now he chose to stay at work, showering in the bike room, sleeping in a lounge chair in a darkened atrium overlooking Green Mountain and the Boulder Flatirons, those mountainous moonlit rock formations jutting out of the ground. At work, he could neatly bisect his situation: the ice-bound catastrophe of his marriage locked behind an iron gate and the silky, infinite blackness of his profession in the foreground.

He heard Erin take a sip of something, and then she said, "I really need you to come over today. This afternoon, sometime today."

With the lightest touch of a fingertip, she shoved the iron gate open, and he felt the cold leaking toward him. "You know I can't, Erin."

It took her a long time to come back with a response. "Because," she said, "today is the day? The event?"

"Right."

"But I thought—" Her tone became more hard-edged. "Didn't you say it would be going on all day?"

"It will." That tension across his ribs tightened. He heard her take another sip and wondered if she was living on nothing but coffee. When she seemed to have drifted, he asked, "Have you eaten anything?"

"Yes." She sounded defensive, but he had to raise the issue because this was what they did now. He interrogated and she deflected.

"What did you have?"

"Muffins," she said. "And fruit."

Not true, he could tell. "Erin, please, you have to eat."

"I know," she said. "I will." But there was no substance, not the slightest intention behind her words. "Couldn't you come after work?"

He would have willingly gone to the farthest reaches to get his old Erin back, if he knew where to find her, his beautiful bohemian. A fragment of the past sped through his mind—coming home one evening to see Erin and Korrie with white clover-bloom crowns in their dark hair, glitter on their cheeks, strings of seashells around their necks, and aqua-blue ribbons hanging from their shoulders. Erin stood imperially on the oversized ottoman, hands in fists on her hips, and said, "'Twas a day of sport for the squid queen and her squidling."

Korrie leaped from the sofa to the ottoman, laughing, and said, "Squidling *princess*." The slightest lisp because of that loose front tooth.

Zac ached with the memory of their warmth hugged against his chest and their hair smelling of watermelon shampoo.

He would have gone beyond the grave to see Korrie again. In fact, some months ago, in a bizarre moment of insomniac free fall, he had thought about digging down to her casket to be sure he still knew where she was.

In the bewildering days before the funeral, he had convinced himself it would be a comfort to inter her at the small, old cemetery that sat just across the road from the lab. Green Mountain. Probably because her death hadn't become real yet, and he'd imagined her being within walking distance— half-imagined her walking across the grass and up to the door of the lab. But of course, he'd been wrong; there was no comfort.

"It'll be late when it ends," he told Erin, feeling as if he were heaving hard to shut that iron gate.

Erin's voice rose again out of the cell phone but with a more urgent, colder edge. "Zac, it's the five-hundredth day."

"You think I don't know what day it is?" He stopped himself. This was not the way he intended to talk to her. He rubbed his fingers across his forehead. *Just let it play out. Let her say what she needs to say.*

"I guess what I don't understand," she said, "is why you have to be the one, and why it has to be all day. On a Sunday."

But that wasn't true. She knew why. "Because," he said, "I have to be there as it evolves, if it goes the way I think it will." He'd carefully explained it all months and months ago, but she apparently couldn't remember now, after everything that had happened. He'd opened his notebook and made a sketch for her, showing how in far-flung deep space, pairs of black holes were caught in each other's grasp, orbiting each other in tightening spirals that would soon end in violent mergers. He told her that as the spirals intensified, the orbiting pairs threw off waves of disruption that rippled through spacetime, warping the architecture of existence.

He sketched for her how the imperceptible gravitational ripples that reached Earth could be measured with ultraprecise atomic clocks because time moves faster the higher it is in a gravitational field. That was how Zac had started building his model, the mathematical model that yielded the staggering prediction that two isolated merger events would coincide. His pen nearly tore through the paper as it scratched down the page, his excitement outmatching his drawing skills as he dashed off waves from those events crashing up against each other, the force so great it could create a miniature black hole.

This miraculous entity would form near enough to Earth that its effects could be observed for its intense, short life. His model suggested that the newborn black hole might form a photon orbit of only twenty-four kilometers and have a life of less than a day, but that would be long enough for it to evolve into its mirror opposite, a time-reversed white hole with an exit horizon into a possible future. He and his colleagues might be able to witness the final phase of that lifespan—its quantum collapse, a wildly tempestuous phase of unmoored time.

Back when he'd illustrated the whole thing, he'd wanted Erin to know that only something as astonishing as these mysteries of loop quantum gravity could drag him away from her and Korrie for so long every day. Erin said she found it intriguing, that it sounded pretty epic to her. He'd thought at the time how she would love the triumph of it if the project succeeded, how impressed she would be that he was the one who would do the interviews afterward, that his would be the voice on public radio, his the face on magazine covers.

Now he told her the only thing he could. "And it has to be me because it's my model that the simulation is built on. The black hole won't be visible, but the sim will illustrate what's happening. I'll have to be there to remodel the math as the data sets come in from the other labs. I'll have to do it in real time so Mark and Jin can feed it to the sim." There was no response. "It's a big deal, Erin, for science, for a new physics of time."

He heard her exhale, but she said nothing. "If it does happen today," he said, "it will never happen this way again, not in my lifetime and probably not in anyone else's either. Ever." After a long silence, he added, "I can't take my phone into the Clean Room, but you can leave me a voicemail. And I'll get back to you as soon as I can. I promise." He sat through the seconds ticking away of her not saying anything. Part of him felt a pang of self-reproach, as if he were leaving her behind, trudging away from the iron gate across a field of ice while she stubbornly stayed where she was, where neither the present nor the future could touch her. But another part of him knew that he had to persevere, to do his work, to find some way forward. "Erin," he said finally, "please say you understand about this day."

And then her voice came back to him, resonant with disappointment and bittersweet clarity. "All right, sweetheart."

She hadn't called him that since before The Day Of. It was her. It was the voice of his wife. "I hope it goes well," she said. "And maybe you could come by after it's all over."

Christ, how he missed her. Her beauty rushed over him like a cold current, and his skin prickled alive, from his face to his feet, as if it had been numb for ages.

Chapter Three

❧

With the phone still pressed against her ear, but getting no response, Erin said, "Zac?" The light in the room brightened, and her phone startled her, humming in her hand with a new incoming call. She drew the phone back so she could read the name of the caller. When she saw the ID, she couldn't make sense of it. She refocused and looked again: "Peregrine Elem." It still made no sense. She stood as she accepted the call and put the phone back to her ear.

"Hello?" she said.

"Mrs. Fullarton?"

Cool, white panic slid over Erin's face. She knew the voice. It was unbelievable that this woman was calling her. Speaking to her again.

"Mrs. Fullarton?"

Erin repositioned the phone against her ear. "Yes?"

The voice came back over the line. "This is Jeanna in the office at Peregrine Elementary." An image of the woman surfaced from a murky pool of memories, faces of those who were involved during the days after Korrie's death; law

22

enforcement—Tom Drake, Rebecca Kincaid—and school officials and this distorted face of Jeanna Rattilson. Erin wrapped a protective arm over her chest. "Why are you calling me?"

"Well—" Jeanna paused as if she were the one who was surprised. "We have Korrie here in the office. And she's running a temp of one hundred one point eight."

Erin flinched from the sting of this woman saying her daughter's name. Her lungs shrank in her chest, and she grabbed the edge of the island's counter. "What?" The world seemed oddly slanted, and she thought she might lose her balance. She looked again at the ID and then put the phone back to her ear.

Jeanna spoke again, slow and clear, highlighting each word. "Someone will need to pick her up. Because she's running a temp."

"Why are you doing this?" Erin pulled her hand to her damp forehead. She couldn't imagine how someone could make this call more than a year later, knowing full well what had happened, knowing the part she'd played.

Jeanna exhaled, sounding impatient, before she spoke again. "Is this Korrie Fullarton's mother?"

"Yes!" Erin snapped.

"Then you need to pick her up," Jeanna snapped back.

"What is wrong with you?" Erin paced across the kitchen tiles. "Don't you know what a horrible thing you're doing?"

The quiet lasted a few seconds. Erin thumbed her ring into place. She narrowed her eyes, sharpened her vision, as if this contemptible woman were standing in front of her.

"Mrs. Fullarton, I'm gonna have someone else talk to you." Then there was the off-key music of being on hold.

Erin's pulse thrummed in her ears, and she couldn't swallow. She had to have water. She grabbed a cup and filled it from the tap. It was then that she looked up through the windowpane again.

Outside, it was snowing.

She dropped the cup, and it clattered into the sink.

Snowflakes chased down from the pearl-gray cloud cover. Half a foot of new snow lay on the ground, and the limbs of the spruce trees hung heavy with the slow-falling burden. She set the phone down and leaned on the counter with a hand over her eyes. *This is what happens,* she thought. *Eventually, you lose your grip and start to fall.*

When the tin sounds of a voice rose from the phone, she picked it up, put it to her ear, and listened.

". . . first name on the emergency contact card, and we are required by state law to call in this order. If there's a problem and you need to update your information—"

"No," Erin interrupted, scrutinizing the snowfall. "I don't—I'm sorry." She searched for the most accurate words. "I'm not sure what's happening."

A similarly sharp exhale. Irritation. "Look," this other woman said. "What's happening is we need Korrie picked up. She can't go on the field trip, and she can't stay in school with a fever."

Erin stared out at the whitened spruces. "I'm sorry?"

"Are you all right?" Still the irritation. Then, after a moment, "If there's a problem, I have to inform you that I will call the next person who's responsible for your daughter—"

Her daughter.

On impulse, Erin dropped the phone on the counter and ran to the stairs and up toward Korrie's room. She froze in front of the closed door. *Impossible,* she thought. She should count to five. Her self-care instructions. *Stop. Breathe. Count. Step back. Break the loop.*

Her thought was to open the door slowly so the dust wouldn't stir, the air wouldn't shatter—the quiet that had accumulated over all the months when she had stopped outside the door and held her breath and listened. The empty room should be just as it was, nothing but dark space; in the closet, the neat white boxes of Korrie's things that Erin's mother had packed up and placed in stacks. For an instant, Erin wondered if Korrie's specter would wake, silver light in the dimness, and turn to her, a stunning, beautiful, living absence.

She reached for the knob, turned it, and flung the door open wide. The riot of color sent a shock through her. Color and light and clutter. All of Korrie's things were back—her bed, tumbled with her purple covers and fuzzy pillows, her turquoise curtains, her lamp revolving with lavender lambs, her clothes, her toys, her games, books, shoes, socks everywhere. The world—as it was supposed to be.

Who would do this? Who could have done it? No one had been in the house but her.

She let herself slide slightly forward into this new illusion. "Korrie?" she said. Nothing. She called down the hallway. "Korrie?"

No answer. *Because you're insane,* she thought. *Could I have done this? Walking in my sleep or something?* She needed some kind of confirmation. She pulled herself from the enchantment of Korrie's room, ran back down to the kitchen, and grabbed her now-blank phone. The school had hung up. The display read 9:35 AM, February 7, and showed snow showers and a temperature of twenty-eight degrees.

Specks of white tumbled down outside the window.

Erin's hands shook. Her mind became a maze. *But it's June now. Not winter. February seventh? The* seventh? *But it's summer, Erin.* She powered off the phone, waited for the gear wheel to spin and go dark, and then she held down the button and turned it on again. The glass face bloomed with the background image of Korrie at Christmas and the date read February 7, 2020; the time, 9:35 AM. Snow showers and a temperature of twenty-eight degrees.

Chapter Four

✎

Erin charged down the stairs at 8:25 AM, struggling into her new dressy coat, with her purse, phone, and keys in her hands, torturous high heels clacking against the wooden treads. According to her weather app, the high would be thirty-nine, and the snowstorm would last most of the day, but much as she'd love to, she couldn't show up for her job interview in her old hiking boots.

Zac was on a work trip to the Hingoli lab in India, and his long flight home wouldn't get in until that afternoon, so it was up to her to drop off Korrie, who stood near the front door, fortressed inside heaping layers of lavender outerwear. Hat, scarf, mittens, button-up sweater, thermal pants, parka; permission slip for Sledding Day poking out of her pocket. On her right foot, a furry white boot from the pair Erin's parents had brought back from their trip to Iceland; on her left, a pink sock.

Erin stopped. "Where's your other boot, Squid?"

"I don't know." Korrie looked down at her sock.

"Go find it," Erin said. "We'll be late."

Korrie didn't move. "I already looked."

"Korrie." Erin sharpened her tone. "We have to go. The roads are bad, and I can't be late. You have to get to school, and I have to get to my interview. Please go find your other boot. Right now."

Within that bounteous inventory of winter wear stood a delicate six-year-old so thin and small for her age that the pediatrician had recommended geriatric protein drinks for her. Her hair was dark chaos in need of a brush. Her cheeks were high pink, her other features eclipsed by the roundness and lucent gray of her eyes, but there was also something stormy on that face. Erin recognized the look. Noncooperation. *And she looks exhausted,* Erin thought; she'd have to check on her later, after the interview. "Go find your boot, please," she said.

Korrie stayed planted in place. "I told you I already looked."

"I don't have time for this." Erin flashed hot inside her coat.

"But I'm having a hard morning, Mommy," Korrie said, the bad mood folding creases between her eyebrows.

"So am I, kiddo." A petulant comeback, Erin knew, but the fact was she was battling against herself more than against her daughter. She would have loved nothing more than to strip off these horrible plasticky interview clothes, put on her sweats, and light a beautiful fire in the fireplace— she was sort of an artist when it came to building a lively, crackling fire. She'd sent away for a new fireplace set and had matchbooks printed with this winter's Christmas picture of the three of them. She could make a cup of cocoa and work on the new recipes for her website. But that was the wrong Erin. Getting too late in the race for all that, as her father had said. He'd finally told her, after all this time, how deeply she'd disappointed him, never having managed to get a degree with all the money he and her mother had spent on her education. He'd pressed her to change, to finally get started on a substantial career, to stop all this wishful thinking. And so it seemed it was time to get rid of this Erin, to wake up and be someone else.

"Let's go," she said.

When Korrie still didn't budge, Erin dumped her things on the chest by the door and took off through the living room. She rattled in her heels up the stairs and rummaged through Korrie's room until she found two black snow boots in the closet. She rushed back down the stairs and set the boots in front of her daughter's feet. "Put those on."

"I hate those."

"Come on, Korrie. Just put them on."

Slowly, Korrie slid her white boot off and stepped into the black boots.

Erin picked up their things and opened the door. They plunged out into the bitter, bright gray, the wind gusting ice flakes against their cheeks. Korrie clomped down the walkway toward the garage as if they had all the time in the world. Erin yanked up the heavy old garage door and didn't try to mask her exasperation as she opened the car door and tossed their stuff onto the back seat. "Today of all days," she said.

Chapter Five

~

9:40 AM
Sunday, June 20, 2021 | 371 Nysa Vale Road

Erin shut her eyes and opened them again. Still February 7. 9:40. Still snowing. To her right, the refrigerator door was plastered with all of the photo magnets she and Korrie had made, pinning the calendar of school holidays for 2020 and Korrie's drawings and paintings. Wistfulness twinged in Erin's chest for those creations she loved.

She rushed to the living room. The scene stunned her. Everything was back the way it had been, before. The pictures, the art projects, the toys, the papers, the mess. She and Zac had fought about it. About how she wanted to leave things the way they had been on The Day Of, and he wanted to change everything. She'd accused him of moving on, and he'd yelled that he couldn't live with all of it, that it was too much for him. And here it all was, everything that had since been stored away. Back again.

Erin ran to the front door and threw it open, and the icy wind swooped in with a curl of snow. February weather. She shut the door and turned back to the living room. In two steps, she was in front of the TV. She grabbed the remote and turned it on. The run-of-the-mill winter morning blather, channel after channel. She shut it off and crossed the room. On the sofa was the sweatshirt that belonged to Korrie's friend Brennay, a zippered hoodie with monkey ears on the hood that she'd left behind when Erin took her home. Had anyone ever returned it? Erin couldn't remember now. The coffee table was strewn with pieces of the unfinished puzzle the girls had been working. On Erin's desk, her computer glowed with the screensaver of Korrie's summer swimming photos, one of her at the top of the slide, one laughing open-mouthed as she slid down, the splash as she hit the water. Then one in new school clothes—and Halloween, the Snow Queen. Erin let the photos cross-fade, one after another, a blissful pang of longing with each one. A close-up of Korrie and Zac wearing Thanksgiving turkey hats Erin had made out of felt for them; Winter Solstice, the lantern-lit sleigh ride with Abby and Brennay and Emma, the four girls bundled together under plaid wool.

Erin leaned over her keyboard and clicked into her email. Nothing after February 6, 2020.

What about Zac? she thought. What would he make of this if she described it all to him? She leveled her phone and touched the image of his face. After three rings, it went to his voicemail, and she heard the message he'd put on his old phone when he first got it: *"No time like the present to leave a message."* She'd barely understood why he thought that was so funny. Something about how the edges of the past and present overlap because time runs faster the higher it gets in a gravitational field.

She disconnected the line and dashed, two stairs at a time, back up to Korrie's room, phone in hand. On top of her purple comforter lay her pajamas. The pair that Erin had sewn by hand, the fabric patterned with pinecones, snow-flakes, and tiny sleeping reindeer. She sat on the bed and picked up the pajamas. Cotton washed into buttery softness. She hugged the cloth against her chest. *What have you done, Erin? Have you finally let it happen? Have you finally let yourself go over the edge?*

Ever since The Day Of, she'd lived with the surreal sense that she was sitting ten rows back, watching herself on a screen, as if at some future point the horrific events of some other woman's life would wrap up, the movie would be over, and Erin would walk out of the darkness and back into her real life, as her real self. But now, here in this room, it was not cinema; these things of Korrie's existed as facts. Erin ran her hand over the fuzz of the pillows. *See? Really here.* She stood and touched the lampshade, then the nightstand, the dresser, the books on the shelf. She leaned out of the doorway and looked down the hall. Through the open bathroom door, she could see Disney towels and winter laundry in a pile on the floor: little sweatpants, a T-shirt, sweater, socks. *You have,* she thought, acquiescing to the idea. *You have lost your mind.*

Heading toward the bathroom, she pressed her phone awake again. *Wait.*

Now the face read 9:56 AM, June 20, 2021.

"No," Erin said aloud. She looked up, and the laundry was gone. "No!"

She turned and ran back into Korrie's room. Dark. Completely empty. Four blank walls. She crossed the room to the closet, and there in stiff white stacks were the boxes of Korrie's things, labeled with magic marker in her mother's blocky handwriting.

With horrible clarity, it all came rushing back down on her. The whole thing. From The Day Of to this five-hundredth day, from that one snowy morning to this awful summer day, the smothering weight of it all landed on her again. Erin backed up against the wall and let herself slide to the floor.

"What the hell was that?" she said aloud.

For these few strange minutes, she'd felt some restoration, as if she had finally escaped through the bars and flown free. Her old life, the only life that mattered, had reemerged and surrounded her, but now it was gone, and she could feel its warmth receding. What a malicious thing grief was, to let her have the only thing she wanted and then to snatch it away again.

After going through her steps of self-care—a stop, a cycle of deep breaths, a count of five, settling her pulse, and reordering her mind—she decided to pick herself up. Get herself straightened out. She lumbered down the stairs, went into the kitchen, retrieved the cup, and drank some water.

Outside the kitchen window, the sun shone in patches through the boughs of the trees, their shadows on the dry ground sharper now. The front of the refrigerator was bare. She stepped carefully toward the living room and looked past the staircase. The mess was gone, and the furniture sat arranged in its sterile order, as if no one lived here. She moved cautiously to the front door and opened it. The scent of morning dust and pine. A hummingbird at the feeder. Dry mountain soil, rangy plantings of an herb garden that needed water. The blues and greens of spruce, pine, and aspen.

She closed the door. Everything was as it had been, as it actually was.

Her phone read 10:00. Whatever that episode had been, whatever kind of hallucination, it had run for several minutes. Much longer than her usual flashbacks. Which could only be a bad sign, she decided, probably deserving a call to Dr. Tanner. But the last thing she wanted to do was talk this through with him. He would ruin it. He would ask her questions that felt somehow like commands. He would circle in tighter and tighter until she had to let go, and this thing that had happened just now would drift up and away like a dream dissipating until she couldn't reach it anymore. She wanted to keep it for herself. No matter what it was.

Maybe she could write it down in her notebook. What a treat that would be for Group. Not only was she refusing to move forward; now she'd let herself fall backward off the cliff. *Cluck.* Concerned clucking all around. She ran her palms up her forehead.

"Damn." She let all the breath out of her lungs. "What do I do now?"

What if she called her parents? She considered what time it was in California, what they might be doing on a summer Sunday morning. She touched her mother's number on her phone and paused for a second to let it ring. But what kind of reaction would it cause if her parents found out she was getting worse? She quickly ended the call.

Her mother still couldn't say Korrie's name aloud; referred to the abduction as "the incident"; never said that her granddaughter had died, but that they'd "lost" her. She said it wasn't Erin's fault, again and again and again, until Erin wanted to ask when she would ever be able to convince herself.

It was probably better not to tell anyone about this episode she'd had. What good would it do to set off a bunch of alarms if she didn't have to? She could deal with this by herself. Maybe it would unscramble her mind if she shut it down for a while. She decided to go back to sleep.

In her bedroom, she tried to make the space like night—closed the curtains, turned off the lamp, and crawled under the comforter. She closed her eyes, mulled for a moment.

"But I'm having a hard morning, Mommy."

The voice in this memory sounded different than it had on the actual day. It sounded more distant. A barb of remorse tugged painfully in Erin's chest. She whispered, "I know, Squid."

Sleep came and went in shreds. She was aware of her breathing, of floating, of falling, of dreaming she was in bed with Zac. The bed was some expansive version of the one they'd shared in Berkeley. They were both young and naked and not quite the people they were really, and her body was like a teenager's, but her belly was rounded in late pregnancy, though in reality Korrie was conceived here in Colorado. Zac spooned behind her, his hand reaching over her hip and cradling the bump. He asked her what it felt like, having a small human in there.

"Like a little squid wriggling inside a water balloon." This was a memory, she understood in the dream, and when she turned to Zac to ask if he was remembering it too, he was gone. Her belly was flat and smooth, and the realization rushed over her that she'd misplaced the baby, forgotten about her. The baby had somehow fallen out. Trying not to lose control, Erin got on her knees and unfolded the wrinkles of bedding, searching for her, knowing that she was very small and hard to see.

Chapter Six

~

Erin arrived at 9:15 for her interview. Fifteen minutes late. She pushed through a revolving door that spilled into the reception area where a security officer told her to sign in, clip on a Visitor tag, and wait while he informed the interviewer.

After a monosyllabic phone exchange, which included a glance up at Erin, the man said to her, "Bethany's on a call now. She'll come get you when she's through." Erin's sense of the game theory behind this move was that she was receiving a penalty. She wondered if the wait would be an equivalent fifteen minutes. Equilibrium.

Erin crossed the stately marble lobby with what she hoped looked like confidence and settled herself in a chair. On a video wall monitor several yards to her right, a regimental-blue corporate logo loomed and then dissolved into a soundless scene with happy actors playing the parts of corporate entities in very nice suits. She compared herself to them, in her strictly rectangular polyester-blend separates, her weapons-grade pointy heels, no jewelry but her rings, no fragrance but soap, hair tamed into a tight bun. She thought her costume probably looked convincing enough.

The wait was fifteen minutes. Bethany strode across the lobby at 9:30 and reached out for a handshake but without conviction, with only a pincer grip of her fingers. Feeling chastised, Erin followed her into a conference room with a stone-surfaced table and concrete-colored chairs. The two of them sat in unison.

Bethany said, "Any trouble finding us?"

"No." Erin smiled in a way that felt too bright, too phony. "Bad roads, dropping off my daughter at school. Not that I'm making excuses . . ." She laughed almost like a turkey gobbling and then tried to shut herself up. "Just the roads. Do you have kids?" Rapport-seeking behavior. She'd researched strategies to improve her odds. She was supposed to establish the rapport of a person-to-person connection before the interview began because theoretically that would influence what came next. Zac had once told her that people in close proximity share the weave of an electromagnetic interference pattern because the ion currents in human heartbeats generate energy fields of about eight feet in volume. But Erin could detect neither energy nor rapport.

"Nope. No kids," Bethany said. She typed something on her small tablet.

Here sat Erin at the crux of the whole thing. The idea was that she should try to be a different Erin, one not so soft, not so dreamy, not so close to the bottom of the food chain. She and Zac had conferred with her father's financial advisor, scoped the facts of their little future until they understood that they would need to become realists. Her half-finished culinary degree would never qualify her to open a restaurant of her own, and her website of original recipes continued to go unnoticed. And so here Erin was now, engaging in rapport-seeking behaviors, but wishing she were home in her favorite spot in front of the fireplace, with her daughter who was so tender-hearted and sincere that Erin wanted to keep her safe at home forever.

A couple of minutes into the interview, Erin's phone started to vibrate quietly in her pocket. Instinctively, she reached for it, but when Bethany looked up at the first sign of movement, Erin froze. The phone continued to vibrate, humming gently. *It could be the school. Or it could be Zac.*

The moment seemed laden with the testing of her mettle. She contemplated nine-hour days in a cube, proofreading FDA Product Information Forms for a mega-conglomerate, sacrificing her identity as a freethinking and unruly food designer, hearth-keeper of her little family's home life. Would she excuse herself and interrupt the interview for a personal matter or would she put the interview first? She watched Bethany's finger hover in midair above the screen of her tablet.

But it could be the school, or it could be Zac.

Erin laced her fingers and rested her hands on the table, giving Bethany the sign that she was ready to continue with the interview.

Bethany asked, "So what attracted you to the packaged-goods sector?"

Erin was stumped. This question was not in her research. She could not fathom the idea of being attracted to packaged goods. Packaged goods were the anti-Erin, the opposition. She rifled through everything leather-bound, dog-eared, and hand-worn on the shelves in her mind: antique cookbooks with illustrations of vanilla beans, nutmeg trees, allspice groves.

"The challenge," she ad-libbed, hoping to make up something better before anything else bumbled out of her mouth, anything else that might ruin this interview.

"How so?" Bethany tapped again on her screen and looked up at Erin, waiting for an answer.

Chapter Seven

❧

"You motherfucker," Jin laughed.

Zac pulled his gaze from the smooth black glass of his own monitor and swiveled toward Jin's dock. In white Tyvek coveralls and booties, Jin sat like a giant, foul-mouthed, middle-aged toddler clad in snowy footie pajamas.

Jin grinned at Zac and said, "Unfuckingbelievable, Fully! You nailed it." He swiveled closer to the light of his monitor. "Look at this."

"Yeah?" Zac stood and tugged at his own baggy coveralls. He rolled his chair next to Jin's, sat again, and centered himself in front of the monitor.

"Ready?" Jin said.

Mark rose from behind his horseshoe of silver monitors. "Just a sec." The oldest of the physicists on the team, he blinked down at his screens with droopy, puffy eyes, and said, "Okay. Yep, this data set is transformed . . . now. We're in."

"Lookie here," Jin said. He tapped on his keyboard as Mark and Zac watched.

Out of the blackness of his monitor, the simulation began to fade in. A vast rippling plain, like an infinite and waveless gray sea, spread from the foreground to the horizon's vanishing point in the background. Slowly, in the long-distant perspective, a dark violet swell began to arch upward out of the gray. As it appeared to move closer, its height climbed the screen and its velocity rose in magnitude. As the wave took shape, its color intensified, the peak turning electric purple now, as Zac had requested because that had been Korrie's favorite color. The wave roared closer, and at its crest, reflections of light formed into small, bright beads like droplets of mercury. As the wave approached the screen's full capacity, duplicate waves piled in front of it, different hues of the spectrum overlaying the image and flashing text for the title of each location, showing where the measurement came from: Hanford, Boulder, Livingston, D.C., Hanover, Pisa, Hingoli. All of the waves coalesced into one stunning spectral cliff face, huge and almost alive with energy, surging forward toward the watchers, showering blazing-white beads at the crest. As Zac began to feel the vertigo of the visual effect overwhelming him, the wave slowed and began to smooth out. Its colors eased back toward dark violet and then, as the surface flattened, it faded to gray as the expanse lost energy, settled, and stilled.

"You see that?" Jin said. "Each location measured that puppy identically."

"Wow." Zac smiled and let the spectacle of the imagery settle behind his eyes. Evidence that the first wave matched the prediction in his twelve-hour countdown. This meant his model had elegance, and the data was confirming the likelihood that a miniature black hole could form in the hours ahead. Warmth flooded in.

Mark looked down at one of his screens. "From all the sites, the signatures align to our sim at ninety-seven point four percent."

All three of them laughed at the absurd degree of accuracy in the result.

"Holy fuck," Jin said, "we've got to get rid of you, Fullarton. You're a danger to us all." With a bootie-covered foot, he shoved Zac's chair so it rolled away, across the white tile of the Clean Room.

Mark sank back down behind his monitors, only the percussion of rapid clicks on his keyboard showing his doggedness as he worked with Zac's equations to reconfigure the simulation.

Zac rolled himself back to his own dock and said, "Pretty cool, huh?"

"You know what would be cooler?" Jin said. "If you could cook up a second time crystal that would tether to this one so they'd become an entangled pair," and he gestured toward the atomic clock. "Then it could ride like a buoy on the wave and we wouldn't have to wait for data from all the other sites. We'd be linked and we could tweak the sim as a wave rolls by, from within it instead of after it's gone."

Zac thought for a second. "Actually," he said. "This *is* the second time crystal. My wife has the first one."

"No shit." Jin tilted his head to the side. "Same frequency?"

"Yep," Zac said. "Same setup. Same frequency. Same everything."

"So that's pretty fucking interesting," Jin said.

Mark interrupted. "Okay, the new data is laid in and we're reconfigured." He hit a double keystroke. "I'm sending it to the big screen," he said as he stood and faced the large wall monitor. The flat, gray sea appeared on the screen, and far against the distant horizon the violet wave began to form. "And this," he said, "is what the next one should look like."

Zac gazed at the screen as the wave rose, light just beginning to glisten at the apex. He let an unfamiliar feeling play across his chest. What was it? Joy? *It's okay*, he told himself. *You can have a little bit.* His hand reached by reflex for his phone so he could call Erin and tell her about this dream coming true, but, of course, he didn't have his phone on him. It was locked in his drawer in his office.

And what if he did call her, after the end of the whole thing, tonight? Went back to the house? Made a late dinner with her, opened a bottle of wine? They could make their special farfalle pasta, butterflies' wings of Italian semolina with marinara and spicy sausage. He could make a salad with feta cheese and black olives, and he'd open a nice cabernet. He could describe to her how he and the guys saw all of their work come together like pinions, jewels, and wheels behind the smooth watchmakers' crystal of the black glass monitor. But would his news somehow breathe life into her again and bring the old Erin back to him? Unlikely. She and Korrie had exited the stage as a pair, mother and daughter.

He wished the Erin from before was still where he could reach her. He longed for her to be there for him, to acknowledge this victory with him, this one tiny blip of relief from their situation, for just one minute before she disappeared beneath the ice-cold surf again like some half-drowned, green-skinned, silk-scaled Nereid. If she had her way, she'd pull him under with her, and he found it exhausting to fight so hard to resist her when all he wanted was for her to ask him to come back home. He imagined pushing her away as he struggled toward the surface.

Korrie, he said silently, *your dad did something cool;* and then from his precious storage of memories, he called up the scent of watermelon baby soap as if she were curled against him on the sofa, leaning into him the way she used to. *You'd be proud, Squid. Your friends might see me on TV. They're probably getting big now, your friends. They'd be eight, right? Emma and Abby and Brennay? Eight years old? But you're still six.*

Morbid thinking, he told himself, *pathetic.* He was almost starting to get past the initial fixations of grief, but he doubted he'd ever get rid of the feeling that she was out there somewhere, waiting for him to get off work so he could come pick her up and take her home.

With a monumental effort, he divided himself in two, and the stronger part went back to the unassailable beauty of the simulation and his friends who understood what it meant.

Chapter Eight

～

Erin woke and opened her eyes, and tears welled as she turned her mind back to Korrie's bedroom. It had been one of the great joys of motherhood to decorate that room and fill it, year upon year, with everything of Korrie's choosing, all the things she loved that made the place her own little realm.

After Korrie's death, everyone promised Erin there would come a time when she could let go of her daughter's belongings, that she would one day feel ready to put them away. But that day never came, and it had been such anguish to watch as her mother did it for her.

And now, something had happened in her mind, as if she had re-created that room again, the way it had been on the day Korrie died. And it had seemed so real.

She shivered beneath the covers, tears running warm across her cold cheeks. She really should tell Zac about her hallucination, she decided, in case something worse happened. He would need to know. He might have to check on her. Nothing like this had ever happened before, and she needed to leave a message so he would call back.

She fumbled her phone awake and touched his image. How could she word this message? *Hey, when you get a chance, I've had a psychotic break, and I can't decide if I should go to the emergency room or just let the show go on. Thoughts?*

The ringing sound went on until his voicemail picked up, but his voice had the lighthearted cadence of his old recording: *"No time like the present to leave a message."* She jumped out of bed. *Again? This again?* What could be going on? She'd hoped some sleep would reset whatever was wrong, as if her brain could reboot and the strangeness would clear out of the system like a glitch of crossed software. She disconnected the call and examined the face of her phone. The display read February 7 again. But now—10:33 a.m.? So it was showing The Day Of—from the past—but in her mind's eye the hours were moving forward just like in any other day?

She pocketed her phone and threw open the curtains. Outside, the snowfall was heavier now, the flakes drifting like feathers. She ran to the door of Korrie's room, nursing some small, impossible thought that she might see her there, but the room was filled only with the light from the lamp and the hodgepodge of every lavender, ruffled, and glittered thing Korrie had ever loved. Erin stumbled down the stairs to the front entry, stepped into her old boots, and dashed out into the storm.

The sky was no sky, no delineation between the light and the cover of the storm, and the air filled with snow. The trees drooped under the weight of their soft mantles. She jogged to the end of their road and looked both ways along Fourmile Canyon Road into the heavy white silence. Nothing moved except the snow. There was no sound except the hiss of a million flakes as they fell. Nothing extraordinary in either direction—except everything.

She turned back and ran toward the house. As she rushed up the road through the frozen woods, she searched for any clue that this strange episode might include Korrie, but nothing marked the new-fallen snow except the tracks from Erin's own boots.

Once she reached the house and crossed the threshold, she closed the door behind her. "What can I do?" She was up the stairs in seconds and back in Korrie's room, the jumbled vibrancy of a six-year-old girl's world. Her heart drummed in her chest.

Korrie had been making valentines, and on her desk were safety scissors, a glue stick, and several hearts cut out of construction paper. The top one was bordered with glitter, and in the middle, concentric hearts swelled outward. Erin hadn't been the one to clear off the desk and hadn't seen the finished product. She turned the valentine over. On the back, Korrie had printed:

4 Daddy. Love 4ever, Korrie

Erin felt its wholeheartedness and tried to keep herself pulled together as she touched the lettering, traced over it with her fingertips. Had Zac ever gotten to see this? Or had it been packed up with everything else? And there it was: the problem. All of these things were packed away. Yet here she was, surrounded by them.

She remembered Dr. Tanner mentioning once that in some types of mental illness, a patient experiences during their waking life what they would see if they were having a nightmare. The interior floods the exterior. Was that what this was? An illness of dreams?

Though she didn't want to do it, she put down the valentine and took out her phone to call Dr. Tanner's office. She would have to tell him about this because he was in charge of her care. He was the director of her so-called recovery.

The receptionist answered the way she normally did, her voice soft yet sturdy. "Good morning, GRT Group. This is Marina. How can we help?"

"Hey, Marina." Erin's voice rasped with the roughness of sleep. She cleared her throat and sat on Korrie's bed. "It's Erin."

"Good morning." Marina sounded removed and cool, though usually she was friendly. "How can we help?"

Puzzled, Erin continued anyway. "I have to talk to Dr. Tanner. I know I'm supposed to schedule time for a call, but I need to talk to him. Right now, if that's okay." She pulled a corner of Korrie's comforter up to her chest.

"Dr. Tanner is with a client, but I can take the name of the referring physician, and we can get your information into the system to get you started."

For an instant, Erin hesitated because this person, who knew so much about her, seemed not to know who she was. "Marina," she said, "it's me. Erin Fullarton."

"Yes, ma'am . . . and we're here to help you." It was as if Marina had never spoken to her, hadn't offered her tea dozens of times, hadn't said she'd see her the next week after each session for months and months.

"Listen to me," Erin said, "I need to talk to Dr. Tanner right now. I'm sitting in my daughter's room, and—"

Marina interrupted. "I understand, ma'am, and I do want to help you. The first step, though, is for us to get your information into the system."

"Marina." Erin pulled her knees up and wrapped her arm around them. "I'm already in the system."

"Well, no," Marina said, "I'd know if you were. But it's no problem. We can get you started now."

"Would you please look me up? Erin Fullarton. I'm in the system; I've been in the system for months."

"Erin," Marina said, "can I call you Erin?"

"Of course." She stopped herself from saying it was what Marina always called her.

"It's part of my job to manage the database, so I'm very familiar with everyone in it." She enunciated gently, as though she were calming the tantrum of a child. "And another part of my job is intake. I can hear your distress, but we can get you the attention you need if we do this one step at a time."

"You really have no idea who I am?" Erin said.

"You're Erin," Marina said, "Fullarton, I believe you said. You just told me that." And she left it at that, as if her patience might be starting to fray.

"But you've never heard of me before this?"

"No." she said. "I'm sorry."

"Even though you've seen me every week since last February?" Erin tried to keep from lashing out at this woman she felt fondness for. "Every week for sixteen months?"

"It's February *now*, Erin."

That feeling of blood draining from the skin washed down Erin's face. "For you too?" she asked.

"What do you mean 'for me too'?" Weariness with the back and forth was beginning to creep into Marina's tone.

"Can you please tell me what day it is for you? The calendar date?

"It's February seventh." Her voice again took on a soft timbre. "Twenty-twenty."

This can't be possible, Erin thought. She stood, and the comforter dropped over the edge of the bed. *It's not just in my head.* It wasn't an illusion, not something that was happening only for her. If it was the same for Marina as it was for Erin, then it was not something she had created. It was something beyond her mind.

"Erin?" Marina said, "Are you still there?"

"Could you—tell me—" Erin stumbled over the pileup of her words. "Have you seen any—anything today when things slipped into a different—when time shifted?"

"Do you mean literally?"

"Yes." Erin surveyed the room, a hodgepodge of Korrie's treasures.

"I haven't, Erin," Marina said.

So it was only Erin who was out of place. *What is it about me?*

"I think the best thing," Marina continued, "would be for your physician to call Dr. Tanner, and I can set that up if you like."

"No," Erin said. Something about her whole world was slipping, and it couldn't be the kind of thing doctors might straighten out. "That won't help." She tried to put an end to the conversation with some composure. "I'm sorry I bothered you, Marina. Thanks anyway." She disconnected the call.

For me, the order of time is out of sequence, she thought. *Only for me.* But how could that have been true? In any real sense? Erin knew that the standard for time was set from the atomic clock at NIST. She ran from Korrie's room, down the stairs, bringing up the website on her phone as she squared herself in front of her computer and accessed it there as well. They matched. The government page on both screens read:

Today: February 7, 2020 Mountain Standard Time
10:40:08 AM

More proof of something. The time she was in now was a different time from the one she'd been in when this day first began. It was a fact she could verify against the same clock Zac had helped create. The one he'd perfected to measure what his model foretold. What if all of this was because of what day it was—the day of Zac's time event?

"Oh my god," she whispered, and she tapped the display of her phone, looking again at the tiny circular photo of Zac. For almost ten years, she had been married to this brilliant physicist who told her all about the whims of time, drew diagrams for her. What was it he had shown her about this day? That the waves would literally disrupt the architecture of time? Something about a black hole becoming a white hole and revealing a new physics of time?

Zac's theories contradicted her common sense, but now her perceptions told her there was nothing common about what was happening, and she couldn't get through to him to tell him what she was seeing. Maybe it was not her mental state that had changed after all. Zac always talked about how shortsighted perception is, how people see time only as their own small collection of memories of the past and plans for the future but that it's a much more complex ocean of probabilities and processes. And now she was somehow swept up.

She ran to the front door, wrenched it open, and looked out at the swirling static of pale flakes. She felt frantic and electric, adrenaline surging through her as she stepped out into the storm.

She tried pressing on Zac's image again. But it was still February, his recording still *"No time like the present."* When his voicemail beeped, she said, "Zac, something's happening. Please, please call me the second you get this."

Chapter Nine

❧

The Day Of: Friday, February 7, 2020 | Pearl Street Office Park

By 10:40, Erin's need to flee the interview felt really critical. Bethany had delved into Erin's documents while she sat there. She'd double-tapped her tablet, and said, "And this résumé." The implication seemed to be that it was a strike against Erin. "This is the most updated?"

"Yes." She'd formatted the document with a large square of color for the heading, giant bullet points, and wide margins to fill the page.

Bethany asked her to describe her educational experience. Erin thought back to those years and then rambled. She tried to shape the narrative of leaving school as an act of high character, the courage to admit she needed to take her own path, but Bethany seemed unconvinced.

"So nothing since Berkeley?" she said.

"Nothing like what?" Erin felt her hopes shutting down, felt less able to pretend that this interview could turn out well.

"No employment." Bethany really seemed to enjoy this part. This fact was something she already knew, but she seemed to have to point it out, just for fun.

"I was going to—" Erin paused. In that instant, she saw herself mirrored in Bethany's eyes, and all of Erin's efforts, all of the busy activity of her daily life, seemed quaint and misguided. "When my daughter started school," she said, "I thought I might open my own place."

"Huh," Bethany's response did not outwardly mock Erin, but there was an opinion in her tone that made Erin feel embarrassed about her unfashionable priorities and the foolishness of her pipe dream.

Bethany asked for written consent to run Erin's credit report, and then she pulled it while Erin watched.

"Do you always do that?" Erin asked.

Bethany lifted her head, apparently cheered even more by the chance to get a look into Erin's financial information. "It's just a soft pull," she said. "It won't lower your score." She flicked a finger to scroll deeper into the report. She seemed to probe it with satisfaction. "Mm," she said.

It had been over an hour since the interview began, and the only thing Erin wanted now was the chance to escape. She wanted to shake off the scratchy burlap feeling of being stuck here with this woman. She let her mind imagine running out into the pure white snow and returning to her stupid little life. If there was a way, she would have deleted her documents from Bethany's tablet and erased the interview from her calendar.

"What do you think," Erin said, "might be the timing now?"

"What timing?"

"How long"—Erin tried to adjust her voice to sound positive—"before we can finish up here?"

"Are you in a rush?" Bethany said, seeming to draw a line to see if Erin would step over it.

"No, of course not." She made another attempt to look eager and bright.

"Well," Bethany went back to her tablet. "I think we should have you out of here before lunch."

"What?" There was disbelief in Erin's tone that she'd been unable to cover.

Bethany tilted her head to the side. "You and I need to walk through an assessment to see how you might fit with our culture; and we have a five-factor model to show where your strengths are. We can compare your results to the team's." A hint of a smile came and went. "All told, that will take us half an hour or so. Right? And then we have timed tests onscreen for you. Literacy, comprehension, proofreading. And that will take us another half an hour or so. Sound good?"

"Wonderful," Erin said.

Chapter Ten

❧

Erin paced through the rooms of their history, wishing Zac would call back. She had to find some way to understand what was happening. She threw aside the curtain that hid the storage area under the stairs and pulled out a box full of his magazines, hard-copy reprints with his articles in *The Astrophysical Journal, Scientific American, Quanta.* Beautiful, glossy illustrations showed crimson nebulae at peace, all twinkle and stillness and quiet. The texts under his name proved indecipherable. These were concepts so simple to Zac that he breathed them like air, but Erin could make no sense of them. Page after page of words, symbols, formulae that meant everything to him but revealed nothing to her.

She found his old laptop and jabbed at the keyboard, trying to get it to respond, but even after she found a compatible cord and plugged it into a wall outlet, it refused.

All she wanted was some kind of summary or abstract that would show her what was happening, some visual something that would orient her pictorial mind to the nature of the thing she was caught in. Or if she could find something in layman's terms that would explain it to her in useful, concrete words.

She gave up on his machine and went back to hers. She typed the phrases "gravitational wave" and "time change." Her search yielded thirty thousand hits. She kept scrolling down through the list as she looked for something helpful.

She saw a link to the NIST website and hit the blue text. There on the menu was the portal to Zac's group. With another click, she found his name, and with another, his face. The photo was serious, studious, professional, his red beard trimmed short, the way he had it before he shaved it off. Beneath the image were links to his publications. She scanned the titles. These were all old articles about gravitational-wave memory. None of the work he'd done recently on black holes. She shoved the keyboard back and got away from the computer.

She walked the floors of their past. Today it was summer, but she was in winter. February seventh. Here were all the pieces of their life scattered the way they were when she'd rushed Korrie out the door so she could get her to school and get herself to her interview. Was she living through a replay? Of the worst day of all days? The last day of Korrie's life?

Somehow, I'm here, in The Day Of. I can see the evidence all around me with my own two eyes. Touch it with my two hands. She pushed the puzzle pieces around on the table. Then an idea lit up in her head. *What if Korrie hasn't been abducted yet? What if I'm actually back in that day, and Clype hasn't taken her yet?*

Her phone read 10:52. How long since the school had called? Pressure closed in. How much time had she blown? If all of this was real, could it be happening the same way all over again? The school had called just like when she was in her interview on The Day Of. On Sledding Day, at 9:32. Her phone said 10:53 now; 10:53 on February 7.

Was it possible?

Erin tapped hard against the glass face of her phone to return the call from the school. It rang once, twice, three times, four. *Where the hell are you?* While the ringing continued, she ran up the stairs, stalked in and out of Korrie's room, up the hallway and back, before someone finally picked up the phone.

"Peregrine Elementary." This was Jeanna, Erin knew, who had no idea at that moment what her part in the tragedy was going to be. "Can you hold?"

"No! Don't put me on hold!" But it was too late. The line crackled with warped hold music.

Erin treaded the floorboards and whispered, "Oh my god, oh my god, come on, come on, please." Somewhere in that school building, somehow, Korrie might be alive. She could be walking and breathing, her heart beating, feeling the effects of a fever and probably wanting to be home. Erin only had to make sure Jeanna could see her, would keep her in sight, and would promise she was looking right at her and would hold on to her and keep her safe. Erin felt herself bargaining with the prolonged seconds of waiting—she would give anything now if she could get it right this time.

But then, with barely a blur, the tone of the light in the hallway changed. The music cut out. Korrie's room stood empty and dark.

"No!" Erin said.

She looked at the face of her phone, and there was no call illuminated. She flipped to "Recents"—but there was only the earlier entry when she'd started to call her mother. She pulled the school's number from her memory and entered the digits. As she rushed down the stairs, she got a canned recording.

"Welcome. Peregrine Elementary is closed for summer break. We will return on August twenty-third. Please remember to read with your student and complete your Summer Reading Challenge tally sheets . . ."

She hung up.

How was this thing happening? What had Zac said? She couldn't remember it all, couldn't think straight. There were supposed to be the waves that he could measure, first there would be the disruption and then the entanglement would become smooth again. Was that right?

She checked the time again. 10:54. She tried to orient herself. This was the twentieth of June, the five-hundredth day. It was almost eleven. And it had happened twice, this thing. So it must have started the way Zac thought it would. And, if he was right, it would happen again and keep happening. That was why he was going to be out of reach for so long. But when the thing happened, it was February seventh, the day Korrie died. *And some things are different,* Erin thought. *This time I answered the phone call, which means the day can be changed, right? Someone can change it.*

She needed to find someone who could bypass distance and time and immediately get to the place where Korrie might be. She pressed 911. First ring, second, third. She found herself storming around the kitchen again. Outside, the trees stood motionless in the bright summer sunlight, and a brilliant turquoise sky stretched clear and clean above them.

A woman's voice answered. "Nine-one-one," she said. "What is your emergency?"

"I need someone to get to my daughter's school." Erin couldn't get enough air.

"The name of the school?" the dispatcher said. The sound of keys tapped on a keyboard.

"Peregrine Elementary."

More tapping of keys. "Boulder?"

"Yes."

"And what is the nature of the emergency?"

"There's going to be—" Erin stopped herself. The emergency that was about to take place was sixteen months in the past. "There's something that's going to happen—" How could she say this? Until the past returned again, everything that she wanted to keep from happening was already long over. "This will sound strange," she said, "but there's something happening with time, it's a physics thing, my husband predicted this, but not the time problem, and my daughter is going to be taken . . ." She stopped again. She sounded like a mental patient. Which is what she was. "My daughter will be abducted if someone doesn't get to the school before he takes her."

"Your husband?" The dispatcher's voice was clipped with urgency.

"No, no," Erin said, "the man who killed her."

"I'm sorry?" The tone of voice completely changed. Just like that. Now there was only disbelief.

"I mean . . ." Erin shook her head. "I mean he's going to . . . There's a time distortion . . . I know I sound crazy, but this is real, and what happened before is happening again."

"Ma'am," the dispatcher said. There was more rapid typing in the background. "This service is only for emergencies.

Now, I can tell you're going through something, and I can get you help. I'll transfer you, and you can explain what's going on with you to someone who can assist you."

"No, wait," Erin cried, "please don't." Wooziness and the sensation of whirling overtook her. She wanted to reach through the connection, almost as if she could grab the dispatcher's arm to steady herself.

"Hold while I get you over to someone who can help."

"Wait," Erin begged.

"I'm transferring you now, ma'am. Hold the line, and the right person will be able to take care of you." Then with a beep, she signed off from the conversation.

Erin paused in the silence for a second before she disconnected. *Who else could she call?* Names cluttered her mind, contradicted each other. *Think, Erin, think. Who can do something?*

Erin ran through the scenarios of what would happen, no matter whom she called. What about Tom Drake? After he had told her and Zac what had happened to Korrie, he'd given her his card. She'd stood there shaking by the sofa, pinching the white card as she looked at the blur of black information. He'd said she could always call him. Anytime, he'd said. She looked in the Contacts on her phone, but she'd purged almost everyone. Only a handful of numbers remained, and Drake's wasn't one of them. She'd kept the card and called while the investigation was still active, but now she couldn't remember the number.

She held down the voice button on her phone and said, "Call the Boulder Police Department." On the second ring, a voice answered—male, senior, businesslike—and she interrupted, "I need Tom Drake, please."

"He's not available. How can I be of assistance?"

"Not available?" she said. "I need to talk to him right now. It's an emergency." She wanted to shake this stranger and show him what was happening, how her fragile little chance was crumbling right in front of her.

"And what is the emergency?" he said slowly, as if he were preparing to write up the details, to hear the whole thing nicely spelled out.

"I just need to talk to him," she said. *Right now,* she thought. "When will he be available?"

"I couldn't say." The officer paused, listened. "If you'll let me know what the emergency is—"

"Never mind," she said. "Forget it."

He started in again. "If you—" but she ended the call. *No time for this.*

On that day when Drake had given her his card, he'd written his cell number on the back. Where was the card now? She bolted into the living room and ripped open the drawer of her desk. She tossed all the papers and supplies aside and looked for the card. Not there. Not in Zac's stuff either. Where could it be? She looked in her backpack, in her wallet. Not there.

She ran out to the garage and looked up at the boxes Zac had stored on the top shelf. They were marked only with the dates from the winter, spring, and summer of 2020. She yanked them down and pulled the top off the first of them and rifled through it. Nothing. She put that one away and looked in another. No luck. She opened the last box, and in this one was the waterproof document bag. On the label, in Zac's square hand, was the letter K. She unfastened the bag, pulled out the folder, and opened it.

Here it all was. Erin felt poisoned by the chemistry of her body's response. Korrie's school picture shone back at her. Bright and perfect and happy and sweet. She wished she could squeeze herself into the two dimensions of the photo, to be there with her when the camera captured that instant of life. She looked past the photo, and underneath it were the pages she could almost photographically recall: copies from the case report, the final report from the attorney general's office, Korrie's death certificate, the deed for her plot at Green Mountain, the receipts for her casket, her funeral, her flowers. A copy of the Order of Ceremony for her service. It was horrific how it all reached out and grabbed Erin, throwing her backward into those early days again. Disorientation, dizziness, suffocation.

There was more. A hard copy of the obituary, the autopsy report, a memorandum of procedure for Korrie's property return motion, which turned out to be only for three pieces of her clothing and the clip from her hair. And tucked in near the bottom of the pile was Officer Drake's card. Erin put the documents back in their bag, turned the card over, and called his cell.

"Please, please, please," she said as it rang.

When he answered, his voice sounded as if he were at a distance from the phone.

"Tom, it's Erin. Fullarton." She stood and paced.

It took him so long to respond that Erin thought the call had dropped. Finally, he said, "Erin."

"Yes. And I need you to do something. I don't have time to explain—"

He broke in and said, "I'm sorry, Erin. I'm not on the force anymore."

"What?" Her mind scrambled for the next step. Should she look for someone else? No, only Drake. Maybe it didn't matter that he wasn't on the force. Maybe all that mattered was that he had been then. "Are you still in Boulder?"

"Yes, but I—"

She cut off the end of his sentence. "I need to tell you something, Tom. You remember Zac."

"I do . . . remember." He sounded reluctant.

"He works at NIST. He predicted these waves. They're changing the order of time. And the abduction is happening all over again."

"Oh, Erin." Tom let out a loud breath. "Lord, I can't do this."

"Please, Tom, just listen to me."

"I'm not the person you need to call." He sounded hollowly serene. "I can't do this. I can't talk to you."

Erin pleaded into the phone. "You're the only person I can call! I need you to get there before he does. Tom, please."

"I have to go, Erin," he said, and again his voice seemed set off at a distance. "Call your doctor. Don't call me. Please."

"You said I could call for anything, and I need your help!"

"I wish you well, always—you know that," he said, and the phone went silent.

"Don't hang up on me!" She watched the screen as the call disappeared and the background image of Korrie returned.

She stormed out of the garage. "I need help!" Her voice fell into the quiet gaps of light between the trees. Even though she was doing things differently this time, she hadn't managed to change anything. The feeling of being smothered descended over her. She had to find someone who would do something, or Korrie was going to be taken again.

Chapter Eleven

11:00 AM
Sunday, June 20, 2021 | 2075 Theseus Drive | Boulder,
Colorado

Tom Drake roused himself. He'd been swamped in a muddy dream until his phone bleated, and some residue of the dream clung to him, a thin overlay of remorse for sins he left behind as he crawled out. He wasn't sure of what he'd said during the call, not clear on what was mixed in from the dream.

He rolled to the edge of the bed and sat up. The watch they'd given him at his disability send-off gleamed on the nightstand. He picked it up and looked at the hopelessly complicated face with the clear dial leaving the innards of the movement on display. Hard to tell what time it was. Eleven? Another day cut loose in a headwind.

He stood and let his frame settle into its center of gravity before he took the three or four steps to the bathroom. In the mirror, he saw himself as the forty-year-old Tom who'd taken the wrong path and ended up looking sixty. He leaned on the counter and examined his reflection. Why were his eyes so red? And his hair looked like weedy stalks. Shower? No shower? When did he shower last? He tried to remember what day it was. Foggy day. Another one. But that phone call. The call from Erin Fullarton. Not sure if he'd dreamed what she said.

He picked up his pill bottle. Paxil, the bottle read, for depression, which somehow didn't do justice to his problem. Maybe cumulative duty-induced post-traumatic stress disorder would have been too many words to fit on such a little label. He tipped the bottle and found it empty. His chest deflated with a sigh. Now he would have to go out. He'd have to go to the pharmacy and get his prescription refilled. He hated to go out, but what choice was there?

He didn't smell great, but he put on clean shorts and a T-shirt and slipped on some shoes. As he walked toward his car, he checked his phone. There it was. The phone call. It hadn't been part of the dream. That poor woman.

He got in his car and backed out of the driveway. When he was still on the force, he'd always wondered how people survived what happened to them. He'd admired them for trying to continue living even when the situation drove them out of their minds. Like Erin. What was all that stuff she was saying? That her husband had prophesied something, and the abduction was happening all over again? Lord. He knew she'd been in treatment, but it sounded like her treatment wasn't working. Or maybe she, too, was out of pills. Whatever, it was tragic. He shouldn't have hung up on her. He turned onto Broadway and headed toward the pharmacy.

The least he could do for her now was to let someone know the state she was in. The world stumbled along outside his windows, unredeemable; or maybe it was that *he* could not be redeemed. But he could call his former partner and ask if he recalled any follow-up about Erin, let him know she might be a danger to herself. Why not? What day was it? Was it Sunday? So he guessed Nate would be home with his family—the little mob Tom missed like a family of his own. No harm in giving him a call. Only to report what had occurred. Anybody would do that.

As he pulled into the Walgreens lot, he hit the number and let it ring.

Nate answered and said, "Yes, Tom, what is it?"

Just like that. No "hello." No "how have you been?" Just "what is it?"

Tom said, "Good to hear your voice, buddy."

"You too." Nate said the words but they seemed smileless, automated.

Tom found a parking spot, angled into it, and shut off his car. He felt heaviness descending on him, the inward slant that triggered his tremor. He had to have his damned pills.

"Listen," Tom said, "I wanted to let you know about something that happened today. About Erin Fullarton."

There was whispering beyond the line, Nate saying something discreetly, maybe to his wife. Then, he said aloud, "So can I get back to you on that, Tom? We're on our way out."

Injecting as much bravado as he could pack into one word, Tom said, "Sure." He let silence close over the space. "I'll let you go."

"Cool," Nate said. "I'll get back to you."

Vague. For a guy whose every word used to be so on point, that was completely vague. A kiss-off. Brothers no more. But he'd known that for a long time.

He lifted himself out of his vehicle and tromped into the store. He hated for people to see him in the state he was in, but there was no other option. People were everywhere.

At the back of the store, a line wove from the prescription window. A conga line of needy people like him, diseased or disabled or destroyed on some level, who just wanted to get their medicine and get home and be safe. Did they all want to go back to sleep as badly as he did?

Poor Erin. *Don't you want to sleep too? Forever?*

Chapter Twelve

11:20 AM
Sunday, June 20, 2021 | 371 Nysa Vale Road

Erin walked the dry gravel path between the garage and the house, turned the other way, tried to think of what to do, and then turned again. There had to be someone to call. Not Zac, not the school, not the police, not Tom Drake. Plodding back up the walkway, she slowed and framed the house in her vision. Here in the midst of bright summer, it seemed like such a dark place, one stone on top of another, like a tomb. Inside it, she'd seen all of the things Korrie had last touched, her reliquary. During those weeks right after the funeral, Erin had been so dismayed that none of Korrie's belongings retained any alchemical trace of life. They were all inert and mute, when what Erin was starved for was some electrostatic thread of contact.

She took another step toward the house, now in summer, stripped of its artifacts, its stones piled around the colorless space where she'd kept herself for all these months, and words sprang into her mind: *What if it's up to you?*

It couldn't be true that this thing, this chance, depended on her. She was the one who—*Don't go there, Erin.* She knew if she went back into that terrain of fault, the danger was that she would wander so far she'd never be able to find her way out again.

Her father had tried so hard to cover his anger at her in the months after Korrie's death. But she felt it. With every stiff hug abruptly broken off, every reproachful glance when she looked to him for comfort. For all his silence was worth, he might as well have said what he felt. *You are responsible for this. You.*

She went back into the house, back up the stairs, and looked into Korrie's room. There was no spectral six-year-old looking back at her, which was what she almost wished for. She stood in the doorway, immobilized.

When her mother had been in town again in the months after the funeral, she'd embarked on a mop-up operation of their life—cleaning, sorting, storing. Somehow, she had found both of Korrie's white fur boots. Erin walked into the room and saw her lowering the pair into a box.

"No," Erin said. "Not those." She grabbed the boots from her mother's hands.

Her mother flashed a look of exasperation at her. "Erin, you have to stop doing this to yourself."

Erin folded her arms over the boots.

"You have to stop," her mother said.

"I can't stop." Erin took the boots to her room, brushed the fur into place with her fingers, and set them down in the closet next to her own shoes. She sat cross-legged on the floor, locked in a loop of memory: *"Where's your other boot, Korrie? Where's your other boot, Squid?"* as if Korrie might hear her thoughts and emerge somehow from between the clothes hanging there and slip the boots onto her feet. Erin had remained transfixed until her mother came and got her and hauled her down to the kitchen and heated up a bowl of soup for her.

Now, Erin forced herself down the stairs and into the kitchen. *What if it's up to you to figure this out?* She stepped over to the island and flipped open her notebook. She looked at the word she'd written earlier and then crossed out. "Same." Aloud, she said, "Or not the same." She ripped the page from the notebook and checked her phone: 11:25. She wrote it in the top third of the page.

On the day Korrie was abducted, Jeanna was the last person to see her, at 11:45. Erin remembered Jeanna making a chopping gesture with one hand onto the palm of the other. Adamant, 11:45 was when she saw her, absolutely. Erin wrote the number toward the middle of the page. So when would the time interval happen again? Question mark. She dug back through the tangle of the morning, looking for the pattern. It was 9:30 when she'd called Zac, and then a few minutes later, the shift had happened for a small stretch of time. *And then again around 10:30, right? And for just a few minutes?* She wrote those times at the top. Was the day moving forward at the same rate in both times? Would the interval happen again at the same rate? Would the abduction happen again at the same time? She wrote *Korrie* at the bottom edge of the page and drew an arrow down to it.

Think it out, Erin. Answer the question.

"I don't know. I don't know," she shouted. "I'm only guessing."

She wrote, *To Korrie first?* and drew a square around the name.

Idiot, she thought, *there's no time for this. You have to get there before he shows up. If time shifts again, you have to be at the school when it happens.*

It was a twenty-minute drive. "Just go," she said. She ran to the door, grabbed her sweatshirt with her keys in the pocket, and flew for the car.

She got behind the wheel, started the car, and peeled out onto their road. She was out of time.

PART II

The Waves

Chapter Thirteen

⌒

11:30 AM
Sunday, June 20, 2021 | Fourmile Canyon

As Erin tore through the winding curves of the canyon, a wild excitement welled in her chest, and she could see herself in the school building, could imagine coming around the corner to the hallway near the kindergarten classroom, could see Korrie trotting toward her as if nothing had ever happened.

"I've been so upset about you," Erin's line in the scenario went, like a dream unreeling.

"Funny Mommy," Korrie would say.

Erin could feel the weight of her in her arms as she held her and hugged her and kissed her forehead. The joy of it was unbelievably light, like gliding. Erin drew a deep breath and concentrated her mind on the speed of the car, taking each turn to the bottom of the canyon as fast as she could without running off the road.

On a sharp curve, with only a momentary blur of brightness, it became winter. Snow hailed down in a thick frenzy, snowpack lay smooth and slick on the road, and the car skidded in half time. She tried to correct for it, but she couldn't make herself react quickly enough and the car continued downhill. Her foot hit the brakes, but they had no effect. She pumped them, and still the car slid across the ice. It slipped off the road and plowed sideways into a drift against the guardrail. The car slammed to a halt. It took a second for Erin to reframe, to see where she'd ended up.

"No, no, no!" she yelled.

She floored the accelerator and listened to the tires whir against their own tracks. She took her foot off the pedal, made herself be still for a second, and then gently tried again. The tires spun in place.

"Okay, okay," she said. She tapped gently on the pedal, just enough to rock the car an inch forward, then with a turn of the wheel, she let it fall back. The car slid deeper into the drift. "Stop," Erin whispered.

She got out of the car, stood in the descending white, and looked at the front tire, buried in snow up to the middle of the hubcap, and then the back, the same. Stepping through the swarm of flakes, wading through the accumulation to the edge of the road, she looked both ways. No traffic, no one to flag down and ask for a push to get back onto the road.

She returned to the car and opened the trunk, but there was nothing useful in it. Nothing in the back seat. She felt around under the driver's seat and found an ice scraper. She glanced at the display on the dashboard. 11:35. Time seemed to have picked up now and was rapidly passing. She took the scraper, ran with it to the back tire, and used it to scrape a clear patch down to the soil of the shoulder.

As fast as she could, she waded to the far side. The car rested in the snowpack against the rail, and the tire was completely buried. What could she do? There was no recourse and there was no time. She rushed to the driver's side of the car, jumped in, and threw it into reverse and gunned it. The back end pitched against the drift and then rolled forward and settled. She hit it again and got the same movement. Slight but some. She gave it one more go before she jumped out and hurried to the guardrail. She wedged herself into the gap she'd made until she could reach the ground around the tire. With the scraper, she cleared the snow away down to the hardpack.

New snow had gathered around the front tire. She cleared that too and then got in and pressed her foot against the accelerator. The car inched forward. She cranked the steering wheel all the way until it stopped, and she tried again. The car sidled diagonally toward the road a bit. Managing her panic, she cranked the wheel, edged forward, cranked it back, edged forward, and did the same thing several more times until the tires gripped the soil and she got traction. Careful to take it slow, she eased the car over the ice and back to the road.

Her stomach seethed, and she exhaled into the cold air. With wet, icy-pink fingers, she turned on the heater and the defroster, gripped the wheel, and leaned forward, trying to see the way ahead. She turned up the windshield wipers, and even as they slapped back and forth at full speed, she could hardly see where the road went in front of her. Her tires slid and caught in jerks on the icepack. *Calm down*, she thought. *Just get there.* She had to take complete control of herself. The clock on the dash read 11:45.

As she reached the edge of town, a black pickup truck cut her off. With a snowplow rigged on the front and hunters' flashers on the roof, it pulled right in front of her. She raised her hand to lay on the horn but changed her mind, because at least while she followed the truck's red taillights, the road ahead would be cleared.

The pickup trundled along in front of her, shoving snow, road slush, and ice off to the side. She followed the taillights, steered within the wake from one slick intersection to the next, to the corner where she needed to turn toward the school.

With a bit of luck, the truck turned there too and cleared the way around the corner and into the drop-off loop. It crept up the drive and braked in front of the school building, where two buses waited and children shuffled in lines to climb into them. Erin noticed how the driver of the truck leaned across his passenger seat to look at the children. On the back of the black tailgate, an oversized bumper sticker read "Honk if you want to suck my dick."

Disgusted, Erin thought, *Someone like that shouldn't be allowed to be here.*

She looked for Korrie in the lines of children, but she wasn't there. Her car's clock flashed to 11:51. She wanted to shout at the pickup to get out of her way. She couldn't believe how slowly he moved. When the truck finally pulled far enough forward, Erin revved in front of the buses, angled into the snowy curb, threw open the door, and jumped out of the car. As her foot hit the pavement, the air turned golden and warm. Summer.

Chapter Fourteen

～

*The Day Of: Friday, February 7, 2020 | Peregrine
Elementary, Main Office*

Jeanna Rattilson looked up at the clock on the wall. From
where she sat at her desk, she had a clear view of the main
office clock and another clock through the glass door into the
vice principal's office; and out the front window she could
see, through the snowfall, the digital display on the Peregrine
Elementary greeting sign in front of the building. They all
said 11:45. It was past time for her break, and she wanted
to get her Frappuccino and her chips and sit in the teachers'
lounge and watch her show on her phone. It was really her
only chance all day to escape from the students. This new
vice principal, Orlaine—*what kind of name is that?*—was
supposed to come out and sit at Jeanna's desk and watch the
phones for an hour, but it seemed to Jeanna that the woman
didn't like her very much, and maybe she was deliberately
taking her time, making Jeanna miss her break.

When the Fullarton kid came up to her desk, Jeanna was
surprised. She thought someone had picked her up already.
The nurse had taken the kid's temp and confirmed her fever,
and then she'd told her to lie down in the nurse's office.

Jeanna had called then, like maybe two hours ago, and left a message for the mother that she had to pick her up, like, immediately. *Who are these parents who send their kids to school sick? Just spread that crap all around to everybody else. Thanks so much.*

Jeanna looked at the kid. Cheeks as red as if someone had pinched them. Eyes that creeped her out, sort of imploring and looking right through her at the same time.

"What?" she said.

"I need a drink of water."

Apparently, she thought Jeanna was going to fetch it. "You can go to the drinking fountain if you need a drink," she said. The kid turned away. "And come right back"—she tried to remember to smile—"sweetheart."

The child walked in stocking feet out into the rush of foot traffic in the corridor, where the other classes were leaving to get on the buses for the field trip. Jeanna couldn't wait for them to load up and get gone. Then it would at least be quiet. She watched until the kid dissolved into the noise.

Chapter Fifteen

❧

Before lunchtime, Aidon Clype pulled his truck into the back drive of the parking lot behind the school, scraping his plow over the snowpack. This was where he liked to come and watch sometimes, where he could see the playground and the fields—and his contract with the city made it easy. As long as the roads and lots on his list eventually got plowed, he could take as long as he wanted.

In past years, he'd had better luck at the end of the school day, because that's when the kids scatter. That's when he could find one who was by herself. But it had been such a long time, and he was tempted to take a look around right now since he was already here.

At first, he thought this day was going to be a dud because he'd seen the kids all loading onto buses, and none of the little girlies were still around. He could see all the teachers' cars in their spots, all snowy and buried, and what a fuck of a time they were going to have digging themselves out—but no kids around, and no teachers back here either. He decided he would sneak one quick look inside the building before he plowed the rest of the lot. He nosed his truck up tight to the curb, pulled down the bill of his baseball cap, and headed for the back door and its nice wide window.

When he swiped away the frost on the glass and looked in, he couldn't believe his luck. There was a little girlie, pretty pretty, fucking fine, right there, all alone. She bent her head over the drinking fountain and got her sweet little lips all wet, and then she wiped the drops away with the backs of her fingers. Plus she was a dawdler. Cute pink socks. He angled for a look farther down the hallway. No cameras as far as he could see. He couldn't believe how perfect it was. He tried the door, but it was locked.

Quick as kaboom, he skipped to the cab of his pickup, grabbed his sparrows, and got his duffel. Dumped all the shit out and shook it empty. Military-size, big enough to fit that little yummy into. All the blood was rushing up him as he thought of how he would get his hands on her. He ran back to the door and brushed the snow from the keyhole. He was glad he had his uncle's pick set, in a cool camo case, his trusty sparrows. With just a worm rake and a malice clip, the lock was open, and he was inside. He was like an Army Ranger—he was that good at this shit. He faked not looking at the girl. She turned and wandered away from him now. Wasn't even paying him any attention. Pretty soon, he'd have all her attention.

He gathered up the heavy cloth of the duffel around the open end, and in a flash, he rushed up behind her, pulled the duffel over her head down to her feet, and hauled her over his shoulder. In two seconds, he was outside. He opened the passenger door of his truck, folded her into the footwell, and raced to the driver's side. Just like that, he was in his truck, with the doors locked and the snow coming down like thick, white blinds. He couldn't believe how excellent the whole operation had gone. She yowled in there, in his duffel, not making a pretty sound, and he told her to shut the fuck up or she'd be dead meat. And then all she did was sniffle a bit, and that was okay.

Chapter Sixteen

The Day Of: Friday, February 7, 2020 | Pearl Street Office Park

It was almost noon by the time Erin was set free from her interview. After she'd completed the stages of questioning, testing, and assessing, Bethany had said she planned to see more candidates and that she would let Erin know if she needed to talk to her again. Erin smiled an overly warm goodbye.

Once she was out of the building, she filled her lungs with the fresh, frosty air. Relieved to be out in the wild, feathery snowfall, she half-skated in her high heels across the icy parking lot to her car. She got in, started the engine, and turned on the heat. With a look at herself in the rearview mirror, she shook her head. She knew she was never going to be hired for that job. She loosened her hair and checked her phone.

There was a voicemail, left at 9:32. "Mrs. Fullarton," the recording said, "this is Jeanna at Peregrine Elementary, and we have Korrie in the nurse's office, and she's running a temp, so you're going to have to pick her up right away. She's gonna lie down until you get here."

Darn, Erin thought, *that was a long time ago.* She'd suspected Korrie might not be feeling well, and she wished she'd simply answered when her phone first rang. She returned the call. "Hi, Jeanna," Erin said as she backed out of her parking spot and drove toward the street. "It's Korrie's mom."

"Oh, good," Jeanna said. "You called."

Erin picked up a hint of sarcasm. "I'm on my way to pick her up," she said. "I'll be there in a few minutes."

As Erin turned onto Broadway, she listened for Jeanna's reply and instead heard sounds of exertion, as if Jeanna were making herself stand. "I don't see her now," the woman said. A rustling sound, like movement of the phone from one hand to the other, came over the connection. "Can you hold?" The line went to the sound of on-hold music without Erin having a chance to answer.

She continued along the slick streets until she came to a red light. Snowflakes fell with little crystalline splats on the windshield, and when the light changed, she carefully proceeded on toward the school. She wished she'd paid more attention earlier, when Korrie said she was having a hard morning. She recalled the time when Korrie was about eleven months old, and Erin and Zac had signed her up for a tots playgroup. They'd brought her home afterward, late in the afternoon, and she was deliriously animated, bubbling with her baby words, and then she became exhausted and grouchy and tumbled to sleep as if she'd been anesthetized. She woke early the next morning with a fever, her first.

They'd looked up what they should do in their first-time-parents book: *"Do nothing for a slight fever, but give comfort and have her rest."* When the fever went up again, she and

Zac gave Korrie a small dose of infant medicine, but all the baby could do was alternate between crying and nursing.

When evening came and the fever spiked higher, they rushed her to the urgent care center in town. They waited beside the tropical fish tank and squirmed in their anxiety, holding hands, rocking Korrie, pacing, trying to quell each other's worry with phrases from the book.

At last, the nurse fetched them and led them into a curtained slot. Efficient and unruffled, she measured everything about Korrie, rushed out, snapping the curtain shut, and then came back with an ice pop and a cold compress. She squirted an orange blast of medication into Korrie's mouth and dismissed them, ushering them out to pay their bill.

Once they were home, the fever started to diminish, and they put Korrie to bed. They both felt a little silly that they'd overreacted, but also like they'd been through something together, the three of them. And they'd sailed on and everything was fine. She and Zac joked about how inept they felt, how scary it was, that first time of not knowing what to do.

Now, on the phone, Jeanna's voice came back over the line, sharp and high pitched. "Mrs. Fullarton, can you hold?"

"I've *been* on hold," Erin said, but Jeanna sent her back to the music to wait some more.

Erin shook her head. She pushed on over the ice and slush, wondering what Jeanna's problem was. She and Zac had chosen this school for Korrie because of its achievement scores and its teachers and because it was located so near to NIST that Zac could drop her off in the morning on his way to work. But if Jeanna was any indication of how people ran the place . . .

A different woman's voice interrupted the music. "Mrs. Fullarton?"

"Yes." Now Erin felt her concern worsening. What was going on? Who was this person?

"My name is Orlaine Corray, and I'm the new vice principal here at Peregrine." There was a frightening formality about her approach to Erin. "Jeanna tells me that we requested some time ago that Korrie be picked up. Is that correct?"

"Yes." This was something serious. "What's wrong?"

There was a pause and the sound of the handset being jostled. "We are looking for her right now, but Korrie might not be in the building."

"What?" Erin cried. "What do you mean 'not in the building'?"

"Mrs. Fullarton, please stay calm." But it was the woman who sounded like someone trying to keep herself calm. "There might have been a misunderstanding about whether Korrie thought she was allowed to go on the field trip." There was other dialogue in the background of the call. "We think if she's not in the building, then maybe she got on one of the buses, and we're confirming it by cell phone with the teachers who are out with the children."

"You don't know where she is?" Erin screeched. She accelerated through a stoplight. Her vision seemed to narrow around her.

"Keep calm, Mrs. Fullarton," Orlaine said, "We just need to wait for word back from the teachers on the field trip."

"I'm almost there." Erin raced past the red-tiled buildings of the college campus, past NIST, cutting in and out between the slow-moving cars on the slippery road. It was as if an alarm had gone off in her head, drowning out the woman's words about adherence and protocol. It affected her eyesight as the world went pale and off-kilter in front of her.

She turned onto the road where the school sat. As she charged toward the entrance to the drop-off loop, a vehicle racing the other way splattered slush and gravel across her windshield, and, blinded for a moment, she drove up onto the curb. With a sharp yank, she straightened her wheel and gunned the accelerator to get over the bump and on toward the front of the building. She abandoned her car in the drop-off loop and stormed through the doors.

In the office, Jeanna stood behind her desk. When she made eye contact with Erin, she took a step back and crossed her arms.

"Where is she?" Erin cried.

"I saw her a little while ago"—Jeanna gulped back her breath—"but not since."

Another woman hurried out of an inner office, with a handset in her hand, and said, "Mrs. Fullarton?"

"Yes!" Erin shouted. "Where is Korrie?"

The woman's face was creased with tension. "I'm Orlaine, Mrs. Fullarton." She thrust out a hand for Erin to shake. Erin grasped it absently. "We've called the police," Orlaine said. "They're on the way." She seemed to be in management mode. "We don't believe Korrie is in the building, and she's not out with the other students on the field trip."

"Where is she?" Erin cried.

"We don't know," Orlaine said with a glance at Jeanna.

"How can you not know?" Erin shouted. She had once seen film footage of an entire shoreline city of skyscrapers ripping apart and disintegrating, and inside, she felt like that was what was happening to her. Korrie was not here. How could she possibly not be with the other children? How could these people have lost track of her? In the footage, ancient gray towers collapsed into clouds of dust, crashing into the sea. This felt like that.

In the time that followed, people kept introducing themselves to Erin. The school principal and assistant district superintendent arrived. The district's lawyer arrived. An officer collected the surveillance tapes and took them away for analysis. Teams of officers arrived with dogs and set up a search. Erin fell apart and pulled herself together and fell apart again. People gave her drinks in paper cups and handed her tissues and patted her shoulder. And yet nobody managed to do the only thing that mattered: find Korrie.

Chapter Seventeen

⁓

Erin's boot came down on the hot, dry pavement. The green expanse of lawn, browning at the corners, stretched to the silent building, where the blaring sun glinted off rows of windows. There was no snow, no truck; there were no buses. No children. No other cars. A storm blasted alive inside her, and she just wanted to scream and scream and let the tempest out.

She ran up the sidewalk and grabbed the door's handle. She yanked on it, but it did not give. Shading the glass with cupped hands, she peered inside. Except for shafts of daylight pouring from the upper level's skylights, the interior was unlit.

Erin squinted in toward the office. Through the second set of glass doors, the desk—Jeanna's desk—sat in dim shadows. Erin had not been here since The Day Of. Looking into the space again triggered queasiness, and she felt unsteady on her feet.

She rushed around the corner of the building and looked into more windows of empty classrooms—bulletin boards tacked with smiling suns and large illustrated letters, small chairs stacked on tables, rows of empty cubbies.

She ran toward the back parking lot. When she rounded the corner of the building, she hesitated. This was the spot where the police dogs had circled on The Day Of and bayed that they'd found that one one-millionth of Korrie's scent.

Erin had been standing in the office next to Orlaine Corray. The vice principal was telling a female officer about the procedures the school had put in place and how, minute by minute, they had followed them. "To the *T*," she was saying. The baying of bloodhounds interrupted her.

The officer said, "They've got something."

Erin, Orlaine, and the officer ran down the hallways to the back of the building. The equipment jangled on the officer's belt, and Orlaine's heels clicked in time with Erin's, like sharp little sticks on the tile floor. The hallways peeled back as they shot through them. The relief that this horrific thing was finally over flooded through Erin, and at the same time she was furious that she'd been put through this, and she just wanted to get Korrie and escape home. The three women banged through the back doors.

On the icy walkway of the teacher's parking lot, two bloodhounds whirled, heads down, yipping and baying and sniffing at the snowpack. But no Korrie. The dogs' handler stood in the flurrying storm and held Korrie's lavender coat in his hand. Erin almost reached out to take it from him. Momentarily, she thought of putting it on Korrie and zipping it up. She scanned the white parking lot, cars hunched under shells of fresh-falling snow, and the motionless playground to her right.

The dogs looked up at the handler, and he gave them the command to track. The dogs put their noses down and whined. They sniffed a path to the curb at the end of the walkway and let out two piercing yips. They spun around each other and sat there on the frozen ground.

"Track," the officer said, and he let the dogs sniff Korrie's coat again. They wagged their tails, looked up at him, and sat back down on the same spot.

Now, in the midday heat, Erin approached that same entrance to the school and pulled on the handle, but of course this door, too, was locked. Pointless. It was summer. Getting into the building now had nothing to do with finding Korrie in winter.

And for that second, she wanted to believe that all of this was no more than a bitter delusion she'd created to cope with the day, to match its significance with a monumental breakdown. It was easier to think that thought than it was to admit she had squandered the only chance she had to intercept Clype before he took her daughter. She confirmed it with her phone. It was almost noon now. On The Day Of, she would have just called the school back and learned that no one knew where Korrie was, that she was not in the building.

The heaviness that descended over Erin felt looming and stony and smothering. She fought through it to head for the safety of her car. She had missed the moment. There was one minute before he took her when she could have stopped him. And she'd missed it. She tottered across the grass, struggling to stay upright until she got to the car. She opened the door, collapsed onto the seat, and slammed the door behind her. Her father was right. Tears burned their way from her eyes and down her face. She drew in a ragged breath and held it inside. It was unbelievable that she had blown it. She locked the doors. Why would her heart not go silent in her chest and let it be over?

For one rogue second, she thought maybe she could go home and pretend this had never happened. Who would know? No one—not really.

Immediately after the thought arose, she threw it aside. She wiped her face dry with her sleeve. She had to find a way to see Zac. She had to tell him. But how could she do it? How could she face him now? How could she explain to him that the dead man who had killed Korrie had her in his hands again?

Chapter Eighteen

≈

The Day Of: Friday, February 7, 2020 | Peregrine Elementary

In the school office, the minutes inched by, and Erin tracked Zac's flight home on an app on her phone. She tried to estimate when he would come out of airplane mode and get her message that there was an emergency and he needed to call her. The longer the hours became, the more difficult it was for her to keep her thoughts straight. An amber alert was issued. Erin's first impulse was to stop it from being broadcast, because then everyone would think of Korrie like those other children, those photos that were years old, those facts going stale, and believe that she was really missing, and it would be a false alarm once she was found, but the process was already in motion. It was minutes later when Erin realized how crazy it was to think of stopping something that could help find Korrie.

The other solutions that occurred to Erin were quickly shot down by her own logic, things like getting Jeanna to call her cell phone again, just as she had earlier, only this time Erin would answer the call, and then it would be different. Or the vice principal would call the teachers on the field trip and they would count the children again and then it would be different. Or Erin would call the landline at home, and Korrie would pick up the phone.

The assistant superintendent called the communications office and relayed the information, then sent Korrie's school picture for a media release. As time unfolded, Erin sifted through the morning again and again, trying to isolate the moments when she should have done things differently. Meanwhile, Jeanna was at her desk, crying her eyes out, inconsolable and noisy, and Erin barked at her from across the room, "For God's sake, will you shut up? People can't even think."

The school psychologist, who had planned a non-student-contact day, came in because the other children would be returning now, and the lot lined with police cars and the K9 teams searching the maintenance and equipment sheds would require explanation. The other parents had been sent a text message notifying them that the school was on lock-down and they should come in an orderly fashion to pick up their students.

Erin was aware of all of these things going on around her, but her body temperature seemed to swing from one extreme to another, her muscles shivering with cold one minute and then going limp as she flushed with heat. Her face was damp with sweat, and she felt sometimes dazed, sometimes acutely focused, but seeing everyone as if she were somewhere apart, watching from a distance. Whenever she stood, she had the terrifying sensation of falling from a great height, dropping at high speed, and she just wanted something to hold on to.

Zac's flight got in on time, and when he called her, Erin tried to be clear as she explained the situation to him. "Just get here," she implored. "Don't wait for your luggage. Just come to the school." He arrived at the office thirty minutes later. Fleetingly, Erin thought she should have felt more relieved when he got there, but he looked so scared, like a child himself, so lost.

He gave her a hard, desperate hug.

"They still don't know anything," Erin told him.

"Where can she be?" He seemed to ask her as if she had the answer.

"She's *missing*, Zac." She felt the tinge of cruelty in the way she answered. As if he were refusing to catch up.

Zac went out into the hallway to call his parents and his brother and Erin's parents. By the time he finished those calls and came back to sit beside her, he looked like a man under the heel of doom, ashen-faced and red-eyed, veins thick at his temples and down his neck.

Finally, an officer herded her and Zac out of the building and told them to go home. Erin wanted to get Korrie's things out of her cubby, but he wouldn't let her take anything with her. She thought she should head home in her own car, couldn't see the point in leaving it there, but Zac insisted on driving them both in his car, said that they'd get hers later. She understood that she was in shock and that some of the things she'd said had been at odds with the situation, but that didn't matter. All that mattered was that the situation should resolve and the feeling of falling should stop.

As they drove up the road to their house, Erin scanned the snowy woods for any sign that Korrie had somehow come home. Trees slipped by, white and still, snowflakes descending to the ground, the carpet at the feet of the trees untouched. A large police vehicle sat in front of the house, and Dan's car was parked there too. Zac pulled into the garage and coaxed

Erin out of the car. She could hardly make her legs walk her forward. Dan and Maggie came out and helped her and Zac into the house. The investigators had finished and were on their way out. They gave Zac and Erin their contact information and left.

Once the police vehicle disappeared down their road, Erin, Zac, Dan, and Maggie searched for some missing piece. Could Korrie have asked someone for a ride? Could another parent have dropped her off? They looked through the house again. Living room, kitchen, mud room, bathroom, upstairs hall closet, bedrooms, bathroom. Could she think she was in trouble or something? Could she be hiding? Could she be unconscious? Korrie's room again, the mud room, the garage. Then later, the garage again, the snowfields around the house, the ground beneath the junipers around the garage, snow drifts along the road. All of the hills until the sun set at 5:30. All along the road until last light at seven o'clock. By the light of their cell phones once it was dark.

Later, Dan and Maggie went out and brought back bags of food, and then eventually they left too. When it was just the two of them, that was when Erin started to see that it was really inescapable. She searched her phone for a call she might have missed, but the only message was the one from 9:32 that morning.

Bethany appeared in her mind, with her finger hovering over her tablet while Erin's phone hummed in her pocket; the actors from the video smiled from inside their suits; the security guard told her to wait; and the car slipped on the ice in the parking lot. And she'd been harsh with Korrie.

"Can you remember anything else?" Zac asked.

She looked at him for a long time, hunting. Korrie was several inches shorter than the kids around her, and they'd engulfed her as they all trudged into the building.

"Nothing," she said.

And he wept and hugged her and she hugged him back from some automatic place inside, but she felt as if she were not quite there. She was within a space apart, and she was locked away, and it was where darkness seeped in from the windows and the cold crawled up the back of her neck.

Chapter Nineteen

~

The motor had been running this whole time. The sun blared down on the windshield, and the car felt like a fierce kiln inside because of the heater Erin had turned on when she'd been driving through the freezing storm. She turned it off, opened her window, and pulled away from the curb and around the dusty drop-off loop.

She had taken too long, and the chance to reach Korrie had blinked out like a flash going off. *What will happen now*, she thought. *Will that day end the same way again?*

It had been a rigorous and peculiar battle she'd fought for months against Dr. Tanner. He had issued her a forward-looking time line. Landmarks in the future that she should aspire to reach because he wanted to teach her not to live in the past, not to dwell on Korrie's end. He'd given Erin self-care techniques to interrupt the fixation, the return again and again that masked what she was really up to when she thought about it. What she was really doing, he said, was picking through the details, searching for a way to change the outcome, something he thought kept her from acceptance and prevented her from moving forward in her grief. A stalling ploy, denial.

But she had just had a chance to change the outcome—and missed it.

Zac hadn't answered the message she left earlier, and Erin understood that he couldn't. He couldn't have his phone with him in the Clean Room once recording of data had begun. He and Jin and Mark would be like astronauts in a capsule, so weightless and intent and distant at this end of their long wait that they might as well be on the dark side of Neptune. There would be no one there to open the gate on a Sunday, no one answering phones at reception. She took out her phone and tried the main number, but she got only the recording that referred her to the website for further information.

She needed to explain to Zac what had just happened. She rounded the corner onto Table Mesa Drive and tried to think of how she would start to tell him, if she could even find a way to speak with him face-to-face. At the stoplight, she paused and tried to straighten out her patchy thinking.

But she knew Zac had doubts about her perceptions since Korrie's death, because she'd let herself get carried away once, and in front of him—not a soliloquy in her own head. It was in May, about four months after Korrie died, and they'd been sitting across from each other at the island in the kitchen, arguing in some ridiculous loop about his return to work full-time and wanting to know what she was doing with her days while he was gone. It was late in the evening and they were tired, and she was holding back from saying that she just wanted him to leave her alone.

Something outside caught her attention. "Did you hear that?" she said.

Zac listened. "I hear the wind," he said.

"No. I heard something." Erin got up and raced to the door. She threw it open. "Korrie?" she called.

Zac stood behind her. "Erin, stop it."

"I heard her," she said, and she ran down the front steps and called again. There had been a cry. Not just the wind. She thought she'd heard her in the distance. "Korrie!" she called into the dark as she started for the trees.

"Erin!" Zac shouted. "Stop this."

She spun around and glared at him. "You stop." But she saw she was scaring him. His eyes searched hers for some reassurance. She turned her back on him, turned toward the woods and listened for a long time.

The wind shushed through the trees on the crest. That was all it was. She'd indulged in a little moment of madness and let herself fantasize for a moment that Korrie was not tucked away in the satin of her casket, but was out beyond the aspens where Erin could find her. It was a little vignette she'd slipped into and played publicly, as if it were real, even if it hurt Zac.

When she admitted all of it to Dr. Tanner, he said that the grieving often do hear the voice of their beloved. They often see what they would have expected to see if the death hadn't happened. "It's a powerful force, the mind," he said, "and it resists the loss."

But on this day, sitting at the stoplight, Erin knew the difference between her little moment of drama back then and the reality of what was happening now. She needed some kind of proof. She wished she'd had the foresight to bring something from the house with her. She lit on something: She could ask Zac about the valentine on Korrie's desk, something that couldn't be her own memory because she'd never seen it, never read the writing on the back before.

Once she turned onto Broadway, it would be a straight shot to NIST, but part of her was tempted to just sail past it and head toward home, where she would not have to see the look on Zac's face when she told him that she'd seen the return of winter and that she had, somehow again, lost their daughter. What magnitude would it inflict on him if she laid out the sequence of events for him, explained that the phenomenon he was tracking was much more far-reaching than he knew, that it had swept her quite physically into a moment in time when she could have reversed Korrie's fate, the fate of all three of them, but that the moment had slipped away. She could imagine the look of desolation on his face when he absorbed this second loss.

She squeezed her eyes shut. What kind of coward was she that she could consider running away instead of doing something? She had to face whatever was before her. Pins and needles ran down her spine with the thought of what might be happening to Korrie, somewhere in the world, somewhere in winter.

She had to know if the interval would happen again and if time would resume where it left off when the frame changed or if the minutes had ticked away while she was gone. Zac would have to explain the phenomenon to her again so she could understand the mechanism at work. She had to admit everything and give him the chance to analyze what was going on. Because what if he could figure out a way to undo what the shift of time had done? It was what he lived for, after all, the time scientist.

She sped the rest of the way to NIST. Pressure beat in her head in rhythm with her pulse. Veering into the driveway, she whipped past the guard station and braked to a stop in front of the security gate. She glanced toward the buildings. Across the nearly empty parking lot, she saw Zac's boss. Walter always acted as if he was some kind of manager of Zac's life, both professional and personal, and even at Korrie's funeral he'd made Erin feel like an underling. He was walking toward the crosswalk with someone, a woman. They were headed toward the main building. Erin leaped from her car and called his name. She started to run toward him, but once he seemed to recognize her, he jogged over and headed her off.

"Erin," he said as he approached her, "what are you doing here?"

Breathless, she answered, "I have to see Zac."

He stood too close, tall and imposing, stern behind his walrus-weight mustache and as domineering as ever. He stopped her. "Not today."

"Yes, today."

"I'm afraid not." He gestured for her to turn back. The woman stood waiting on the far side of the lot.

"You don't understand—"

He cut her off. "You're upset. I can see that."

She started to interrupt, but he shushed her and said, "I'll tell him to call you, but you can't be here now." He looked at her in a way that made her feel like an inferior species. "What he's doing is something truly important."

"What *I* have to tell him is important. I have to talk to him right now." She moved to step around him.

He raised his arms to stop her. "No, no, no. You're not going to make a display of yourself. Especially not in front of her." He gestured toward the woman. "That's Anna Schacht, our director and the purse strings for everything that happens around here."

"Just listen to me." She tried to control each word, tried to make herself sound rational. "Maybe you can understand why it's happening. Our daughter is— What happened to our daughter is happening again. Because of this thing." She waved an arm into the sky.

"Right," he said dismissively

"I'm serious, Walter," Erin said in a louder tone. "I've seen it. It shifts to winter and it's the day our daughter died. *Time* shifts. It must be about the event Zac is tracking."

Walter scoffed. "Okay, Erin, you need to run along home." He stepped forward and herded her toward her car. "I'm sorry for you. I really am. But we are trying to peel open reality today. And you—" He shooed her to the door of her vehicle. "You *cannot* make your husband look bad."

She pleaded, "Walter, I'm trying to tell you— What's happening today is—please, please let me tell Zac—"

"No." His word stomped hers out. "I'll tell Zac you want to talk to him." He frowned down at her. "I will have to have you escorted off the property if you won't leave on your own."

Erin stepped back from him. For a second, she saw herself the way he must have seen her—unstable, unpredictable, insignificant. She knew he would never in a million years let her into the building. She glanced toward the woman, hoping for an indication that she might help, but the woman was looking down at a phone she held in her hand.

While Walter stood with his hands in his pockets, watching her, Erin got in her car and slammed the door. She backed past the guard station and turned the car around.

In her rearview mirror, she glared at the reflection of Walter trotting back toward the woman.

The daylight blinked bluer for a second, and then the sky grayed and flooded with snowfall. She sat alone outside the lot crowded with cars mounded over with heaps of white. Flakes showered in through the open window before she could close it. She checked her phone. February 7, 2020, 12:32 PM. She laid the phone on the seat. At this moment of time past, Zac was asleep in an Air India Dreamliner. She pictured him stranded in the air at about thirty-seven thousand feet, somewhere out of reach over the Bering Sea.

She was not crazy, and she would not surrender, but she was on her own, and time was vanishing.

"Be logical," she whispered to herself, "and find an answer."

If there was the slightest chance that Korrie still existed somehow, Erin had to get her head together and go find her. Wasn't that the only thing she could do? She'd exhausted all other options. Focusing her mind, she turned the car onto the street, blasted into the frenetic whiteness, and skidded down the dark strip of icy road.

Chapter Twenty

◞

Sunday, June 20, 2021 | National Institute of Standards and Technology

Zac thought Walter seemed uncharacteristically quiet as he suited up in Tyvek and joined him, Mark, and Jin in the Clean Room, where they waited for the sim to reload. There was something paternal, protective, about the way Walter brought him a no-spill cup of peppermint tea and positioned himself next to his dock. He even put a patriarchal hand on his shoulder, but he was nothing like Zac's father, and Zac wished his father could be here now to see this day unfold.

When he was four years old, Zac announced that he wanted to be a paleontologist, like his daddy. His mother used to brag about how dazzled people were that Zac could even pronounce the word at such a young age. His earliest memories were of weekends when his father took him to the Berkeley campus, to the storage rooms in the basement of the Campanile bell tower, where they would rummage through decaying wooden drawers to find the next relic. Then, together, they would walk back to the Life Sciences Building, and Zac's father would lift him onto a stool in the fossil prep room. Zac remembered an afternoon when his father put a plate of rock under a bright lamp on the table.

"He's embedded," he said, "but we can let him out." He took a dental probe and started loosening grains of rock from the matrix. "You see?" he said, pointing at the outstretched ridges. "Can you see the fingers?" Zac could. The fossil skeleton was that of a prehistoric bat the size of an adult's hand. *"Icaronycteris,"* his father said. "Icarus, the night flyer."

Now, in the Clean Room, Walter broke into Zac's reminiscence and pointed to his monitor. "It's coming in now." He stood. "Let's see it on the big screen."

Jin keyed in the command and then parked himself on the other side of Zac. Mark stood at his dock and said, "This should be it."

On the screen, the simulation faded in. The vast undulating gray sea came into focus, and, far off toward the horizon, a violet wave began to rise.

A thrill ran down Zac's spine as the wave swelled, its momentum steady as it reached toward them. The hue of the wave started to brighten into a glossy electric purple, and its crest shimmered with beads of light beginning to crystallize at the peak.

"This is new," Walter said. "What's with the white reflections there? Are we doing ornaments?"

"Not ornaments," Mark said. "That's how the sim interprets a metaphor for consciousness."

"Seriously?" Walter turned to face him. "What are we doing?" He made a tick of annoyance at the back of his throat. "Are we making this an entertainment?"

"An entertainment?" Jin said in self-defense.

Mark jumped in quickly. "Jin and I agreed that for the sim to be absolutely true, we had to account for the way human consciousness interacts with wave-function collapse when we observe."

"Zac's math does that by itself, without all this extraneous ornamentation," Walter said.

Mark drew in a lungful of air. "The math doesn't illustrate this"—he pointed at the flutter of mercury beads forming in the image—"the way quantum entanglement draws our consciousness, our emotion, into the interaction."

"I know what it's supposed to show," Walter said. "I just disagree."

Zac rotated his chair. "Disagree with what?"

Walter stuffed his hands into the pockets of his coveralls. "With the prettification of science. I don't think adding this kind of thing helps our case."

Jin shook his head. "The sim has to translate raw data and render it visually so we can see what's happening. It can't help it if it's pretty."

"Those so-called ornaments are . . . us," Mark said. "It's the best the sim can do to translate the metaphor."

"All right," Walter said, "that's one philosophy."

Zac focused on the screen. A second wave grew in the background. The newcomer reared up and charged toward a collision point. As both swells rose and morphed into galvanic purple, different hues of color stacked into the space, creating a shifting iridescent spectrum like an oil slick pattern on the face of the waves. At their crowns, the mirrored beads fired in rolling electrical bursts of successively greater intensity. The enormous spectral waves nearly overtook the dimensions of the screen, and in the final moment, they slammed face against face, and the image burst into a blaze of colors swirling, splintering fragments forming lines that ended in crackling, light-spitting points like sparklers that then zoomed inward and locked into a radiating wheel around a central pinpoint.

"There's the black hole!" Mark said.

The wheel shrank inward in an instant, all the lines seeming to turn inside out. They contracted into a tiny black dot hovering in the middle of the screen.

"Wow!" Walter said. "We have it! It's there!"

The wavering gray pattern of the spacetime sea faded in around the black dot and slowly began to stretch and circle with the instigation of the black hole's rotation.

"Incredible," Walter said. He turned to Mark. "Tell me how good the relationship is."

Mark entered a series of keystrokes. The four men fidgeted, waiting for the answer to resolve. "Our sim . . . established the angle of collision at ninety-one degrees, which matches the other data sets . . ." One more keystroke, and Mark said, "At ninety-nine point six eight percent. Ladies and gentlemen, we have a bouncing baby black hole."

The guys cheered. Walter smacked his hands together. "You were spot on, Zac! You said it would happen, and it did!"

"Whew!" Jin laughed. "It stinks like a fucking paragon in here, doesn't it?" He gave Zac a brotherly slug on the arm and turned to Walter. "And you wanted to send him back to India again."

The men fell into uncomfortable silence. India was where Zac had been in the weeks leading up to Korrie's abduction. The trip was part of the idea that he would be the fresh-faced genius who would draw attention to the U.S. contribution to the project, that he would team with his counterparts in India as their facility came online. Walter had pushed him hard to step up, even if it meant being gone for weeks. Zac had harbored qualms about the politics of it and about being away from home for Korrie's birthday, but eventually, he'd accepted the promotion. Walter had said something about how the needs of science could not be sacrificed for the quotidian comforts of animal existence. *And thus,* Zac had thought, *the man remains self-contained and unencumbered.*

Zac had confided in the guys about his struggle with the idea that if he'd come home sooner from Hingoli, or if he'd never gone in the first place, things might have been different. As it turned out, his flight home arrived just after Korrie was taken.

Jin softened the awkwardness. "I think this calls for something spectacular. I might have a protein bar over there somewhere." The guys chuckled lightly. "Seriously," he added, "this is truly mind-blowing. Maybe we should all say to hell with it and spring for a bag of pretzels." Zac appreciated the way Jin was trying to restore the balance as he retreated to his dock.

Zac focused his mind on the stunning nature of the thing in front of him—the spinning black dot in the center of a field of spacetime—the fact that because of what was happening today, the universe made more sense now than at any time since Einstein.

Walter took a seat and started ticking off steps on his fingers. "So next," he said, "a time line. I can do all of the media."

Briefly, Zac felt his own time line zoom into focus. He recalled that evening when he was a kid with his dad at

Berkeley. They'd locked the prep-room door behind them and then stopped in the upper atrium so Zac could lean over the railing and look down to the ground floor where the massive T-Rex mount stood a story high, and he could almost reach the wing tip of the soaring pteranodon suspended above it.

"People are always impressed with the big ones," his father said, and it would take until now for Zac to understand why his father had sounded so sad when he said it. He spent decades preserving the least flashy specimens in the collection and going without recognition, because he was a quiet man who wouldn't crow about himself.

Zac's father was a man of few words, whereas Walter was a man of several thousand. He could launch into a monologue from which there was no escape. He talked everyone into submission. "But first, Schacht," he was saying, "I suppose there's no way to show her a stripped-down version of the sim . . ."

As Walter began to hammer his mark onto the guys' accomplishment, Zac was swept with nostalgia for his youth with his father. He wished he could go there now. When Zac was seven, he and his father went to see *Jurassic Park* on its opening day, and Zac was spellbound. There was nothing he wanted after that but to live on that island and experience firsthand the terror and beauty of those creatures he loved more than anything.

A few weeks later, he plunged into a deep despair that it could never be real. Over time, he developed a belief that soothed him: the view that as the decay of the universe accelerated, it would bring closer its eventual collapse inward on itself until the whole thing would start fresh and the dinosaurs would be reborn.

"Yes," his father said, "wouldn't that be amazing? But time is tricky. You can't know what mischief it might get into."

Eventually, Zac changed direction. He knew how difficult it was for his father to watch as he drifted away from paleontology and toward physics and the science of time, but when he talked to his father about his future, the advice his father gave him was to pursue whatever kept him up at night. Then, he said, it would be like celestial navigation; no matter what happened on the open ocean, he'd know he was headed in the right direction.

Now Walter barged into Zac's reverie. ". . . for another analyst on my grant," he was saying, "We can have a quick call with Burke at Defense and then with CalTech. If you want, you can be on that call."

"Wait," Zac interrupted, "what are you talking about?"

"Making the announcement, getting more people," Walter said, "and more money." He sat with his hands in a triangle in front of his chest. "First, I'll run some numbers."

"But we're getting ahead of ourselves," Zac said. He felt unnerved by the way Walter was pouncing, taking this stunning moment and tainting it with his ambition. "We haven't even reconfigured yet. The black hole isn't even an hour old."

"We've got enough to start."

Zac's voice formed an angry edge. "To start what?" In his peripheral vision, he saw Mark and Jin look over from their monitors. "This was the moment of formation. What about its evolution? What about what comes next?"

Jin angled himself in his chair, looking uncomfortable. All that was visible now of Mark was the dome of his cap.

Walter squared himself as he faced Zac head-on. "What exactly are you worried will happen?" Before Zac could answer, he continued, "You're just a worrier. Okay. But the math is solid." He pointed to the image of the sim at rest, the black hole spinning, spacetime softly rippling on the screen. "There's all you need to see to know that."

Zac's father stepped out of the background and into the forefront of his mind. *"Time is tricky. You can't know what kind of mischief it might get into."*

Zac had never felt such strong conflict with Walter before. He had always let him take the lead, but now he had to oppose him. "I need us to wait," he said. "We have to see what happens."

Walter looked toward Jin and then over at Mark. Neither raised their eyes to meet his gaze. "I suppose," Walter said, somewhat deflated. "We can wait. Schacht can wait. We'll see what happens."

"Thanks," Zac said. "Good." And then after another moment, he said, "Thank you" again. There was something familiar about Walter's disappointment, something that made Zac feel juvenile. He pushed back against it. Walter was not the man his father was. Not even close.

"Hey," Jin said. He sent something to the big screen. A GIF appeared, a looping clip of a cartoon cat, pacing. "This is you, Fully." He and Mark laughed, and Walter cracked a smile. The Clean Room became placid again, the surface glassy and untroubled.

Chapter Twenty-One

~

Erin skidded along the snow-packed roads, unable to think through the fog of the quandary, infuriated and on the verge of screaming or crying, not knowing where she was going. She stopped when the road dead-ended into a deserted lot on the shore of Valmont Lake. She watched a pair of geese settle on the thin ice that ringed the water, wind ruffling their feathers.

She had to go find him. Clype. Her hands tightened on the wheel and turned white. The hatred she'd worked so hard to resolve began to take shape again. It had burned through her and turned her inside out, and now it was back. She had to go find the man she hated more than she'd ever thought she could hate anyone. She had to find him and, so, find Korrie.

"What do I know for sure?" she said aloud.

She knew that this winter interval was the fourth one she'd been through. Zac had said he would be involved with the phenomenon for the entire day, so it seemed probable that there would be more shifting back and forth.

She had the few facts Tom Drake had given her as he updated her about the investigation, and now it helped her feel stronger to put her thoughts in order. She knew where Clype had taken Korrie from. She'd eventually learned that he'd kept her with him and driven around the city until mid-afternoon, and then he'd disappeared. No one knew what happened in the time between that point and the next day when Korrie's body was discovered in Boulder Mountain Park near a hiking trail. The autopsy showed that Clype had poisoned her with oxycodone, the residue of the red pills still in her stomach. After the investigation ended, Korrie's file was closed, and the missing pieces were never found. Very little was known about her final hours except that he'd given her the pills three to four hours before her breathing and her heartbeat stopped. She'd died sometime around nine o'clock at night. Her body had been moved to the place where it was found the next day, but the investigators never found out where she had been moved from, because Clype had died a short time later and taken all those facts with him.

So Erin did not know where Clype was taking Korrie now. All she knew was the area where he'd left her. That was all she had to go on.

She stiffened her resolve, turned the car around, and drove out of the lot. With a shift in the light like the change to a different key in music, summer returned. In one sense, she felt grateful to be back in the time where she belonged, but she also felt the perplexity that she was months and months farther from where she had to go.

Everything Tom had told her was still stored in her mind, though Dr. Tanner had tried to direct her away from all of it because it set her back to imagine the thousand ways things could have been different. Korrie's body had been discovered by two cross-country skiers. They'd been heading south from Realization Point. The snow had let up, the air was clear. They crossed an old mining road and started down a slope when they saw her.

There had been a phase in Erin's grief when she'd let herself get lost in private fabrications of what she wished for. In one of these, she had almost wanted to meet the skiers. She'd imagined herself sitting with Tom Drake, interviewing the two of them, Camille and Brandon. She wanted to ask the young woman how she'd known it was Korrie. Was there some presence she'd sensed there? Had she felt something? But when Erin ran through it in her mind, it was obvious it was merely resistance. In the imagined interview, she might have asked about the other vehicles Camille and Brandon could have seen before they left the parking area. She would have gently inquired about the schedule the two of them had followed that day and whether they could have gotten there earlier. Because if they'd only gotten there sooner— then what? No matter when they found her, it was already too late. That's how the daydreams always ended. Too late.

Now, with only a small handful of facts, Erin turned her mind to where she had to go. She needed to head back toward Flagstaff. That would get her to Realization Point, and she could search from there for the old mining road the skiers had passed. Tom Drake told her it had been closed to traffic long ago when the mine was shut down. So that was what she had to find. Once she was there, it would be winter, and she could search for the man who had her daughter.

Chapter Twenty-Two

～

The Day After The Day Of: Saturday, February 8, 2020 | Boulder Mountain Park

A couple of cross-country skiers had discovered the body of a child at approximately 1:00 PM. Tom Drake had been sent to Boulder Mountain Park to respond, and he was going to be the first officer on scene.

He checked himself in his rearview as he set out, and he looked okay, but he was in no way ready for this. After eight weeks of medical leave, he'd thought he'd have his police powers restored and then be a house mouse for another eight weeks, but they'd sent him out on this call on his second day back. They probably didn't have the slightest idea how he would react to it.

Nobody knew about him; but everybody knew. That was the thing of it. Cops either had to grow a cynical gallows sense of humor or the job would ravage them, and Tom had been deteriorating for a long time, continually battered by what the priests in catechism had called "sins that cried to heaven for vengeance," malice and depravity, when what he hoped for was mercy and salvation.

Nobody knew what it had meant to him that a creeper had slipped away from him. It had happened at the end of summer when he'd been called to the children's story time at the library because an adult male was loitering, setting off the library staff. Tom arrived to a room filled to capacity with children sitting cross-legged and silent. At the back of the stacks stood a disheveled male in his thirties, eying the children. What Tom saw was the man's appetite. He looked ravenous. Tom started toward the individual and made eye contact with him, but then his body overreacted and he charged toward the man. The entire roomful of children got spooked and flittered up like leaves in the wind. Tom couldn't make his way through their pandemonium, and the man decamped out a rear exit. Tom made his way around the children and burst out the door, but the man was gone. He looked for him but never found him.

Tom wrote up the report as a simple "be on the lookout," but in his heart, he believed he'd brushed up against someone truly malevolent and then let him run loose in a world of innocents. A few days later, a child went missing from the Pearl Street Mall and was never found. Tom's symptoms deepened then, and he worked hard to hide them from Internal Affairs. Even so, everybody treated him like an invalid because they could tell there was something wrong with him, even if they didn't know what it was.

At the end of his leave of absence, he'd paid five hundred dollars for his One-Day Test Out in Commerce City. The testing was on a rare day when his shakes were under control.

If it had been on a different day, he might have failed the whole thing.

Now he was back on the job, and the irony was not lost on him that he'd been the one to get this call. The snow had stopped falling. The white hills were unblemished, and the sky was cloudless. He approached the scene at the juncture of an abandoned mining roadway and the Bluebell Trail. The couple who had made the discovery waited in the crisp sunshine.

Tom identified himself. The skiers acknowledged him and directed him down the hillside. Perhaps twenty paces off the side of the trail, in a semicircle of ponderosa pine, lay an army-style duffel bag half buried in snow. He told them to stay where they were, and he followed the tracks of their skis toward what he believed would be the body of Korrie Fullarton, age six, reported missing the day before.

The minor quaking he'd fought to control on the way there was now a full-out tremor. It made it difficult to snap on his pair of rubber gloves. He scanned the fresh snowfield for evidence, but he saw nothing as he approached the duffel bag. Treading carefully, trying not to disturb the immediate surroundings, he proceeded until he stood next to her. There was no movement.

He knelt and looked at the top of the bag. It was closed tight with a drawstring, and the cord was tied in a bow. Two loops tied like rabbit ears, even length on both sides, carefully straightened. *Who does something like that?* Tom thought. He used the camera on his phone to photograph the knot and then untied it. The top of the bag fell loose and revealed fine, dark hair. He pulled down the cloth and exposed the face.

Eyes half open and dark with dilation, corneas clouded, lips slightly parted and tinged blue. The girl whose photo he'd seen. Korrie Fullarton.

A piercing sensation drove into his chest. He despised this world. He reached out his trembling hand and touched her icy cheek. He put two fingers to her carotid artery, knowing there would be no pulse. Just doing it because he had to.

He looked again into those eyes, and he wished he could feel some trace of spirit, almost as if a small bird had been caged there in the cold. As all of his symptoms returned, hammer and tongs, he wished he could shelter her somehow. He felt his heartbeat flickering faster, and he swore to get justice for her if he could.

It drained his strength to have to stand again and step away from her. He used his lapel unit to radio the pronouncement and call for the medical examiner. With all due caution, he retraced his steps back to his vehicle.

The skiers, both of them emotional but determined to be helpful, were college students—Camille Moore and Brandon Evans. Tom gripped his pen and notepad and wrote down their information. They had come to the slope where the trail crosses the old roadway. They'd approached the bag until they were close enough to tell what they were looking at, the outline draped in olive drab and laid out in the white depression beneath the trees. Her boyfriend had stayed at the crossing while Camille skied east on the trail until she got close enough to town to get cell phone service. She called 911 and skied back, and that's when Tom got there.

"Did you touch anything?" Tom asked.

"No," the young man said. "We saw it from the trail, and we didn't know what it was."

"I knew," the young woman said. She told Tom she knew the second she saw it—the shape and size, because of the coverage on the news the night before.

Her boyfriend looked at her and nodded. "So we went a little closer so we could see." He looked at Tom with an expression of miserable disbelief. "But we didn't touch it."

Two more police vehicles arrived, and Tom directed the officers to secure the scene. Two detectives and a news crew showed up, and then about ten minutes later, the coroner pulled up in her van. Rebecca and her team got out and looked out over the terrain. Tom was glad to see her. She was the new coroner now, and Tom hadn't run into her for months. The two of them had gone out a couple of times back in the day, once just for a casual lunch, once to The Bitter Bar where they got sloshed on one Kiss the Sky after another. But nothing had ever come of it, no matter how Tom wished it had.

When she walked up to him, it seemed like a warm greeting when she said his name. "Drake."

"Beccs," he answered, and he tilted his chin in the direction of the body. "It's her."

The sadness of the fact swept over her face, and she said, "We'll have a look."

She and her techs slowly worked the scene, taking photographs, collecting samples, examining the body, and, in the end, lifting the little shape into a body pouch and loading it into the van.

Rebecca returned to him and asked him to sign the chain-of-custody document. Her demeanor was darker now.

"I don't have a cause of death," she said, "but it was definitely last night."

Tom nodded. He felt as if he needed to hide, before she could see what he was like now.

"I didn't see any wounds," she continued, "but her hands are bound with plastic ties."

He felt the involuntary tightening of his jaw, and he reached for his sunglasses to cover his eyes so she wouldn't be able to read him, to see him for what he was.

Chapter Twenty-Three

⁓

The Day Of: Friday, February 7, 2020 | Valmont and Left Hand Ditch Road

Aidon had already decided fuck it and fuck his pain-in-the-ass job—he had a present to open. He'd been trying for more than an hour to track down his buddy with the best shit, but no luck, so he had to resort to his backup plan. He pulled his truck up on the wrong side of the street and laid on the horn until his cousin came out. Gareth scampered from the crumbling trailer through the unshoveled snow and into the street like a fucking priss. Before Aidon could even get his window rolled down, Gareth said, "You woke me up, man."

"Tough shit, dipwad," Aidon said. "It's one fucking thirty in the afternoon, and I need some party supplies."

"Where's the party at?" Gareth said, grinning like a shit-eater, breathing steam as snowflakes landed on his shoulders.

Aidon didn't want to share any info with him, but he didn't want him to clam up and hold out on him either. "The hideout."

"You shitting me? You still going up there?" Gareth pulled his collar up around his bony neck. "What time?"

"No, I need my shit right now." Aidon tapped his fingers on the outside of the truck's door. "And you're not invited. It's only me and the lady."

"What lady?" He sounded like he thought it was a lie.

"Fuck you," Aidon said.

"Fuck you yourself, Aidon."

He hated the fucking little wuss. "I need oxy."

From inside the duffel, his little pretty made a low crying sound, and his cousin tried to look into the truck. Aidon blocked his view, turned on some music, and said, "And a bottle of Jack. And some cherry Coke. Chop-chop."

With a shrug of his shoulders, Gareth waded back into the trailer. Aidon kept checking the road ahead and behind, just in case. It took Gareth a long time to come out again. He finally picked his way through the snow, high-stepping like a fucking faggot, and handed over the bottles, and then he started to squeeze a pill out of a flat, silver blister pack.

Aidon grabbed the whole pack. "I need all these."

"No way, you asshole." Gareth tried to grab them back, but he was too slow. "You gotta pay me, man."

Aidon punched a dent in Gareth's chest and listened to him cough. "Fuck yourself, you shitpile."

"You owe me, Aidon!" Gareth rubbed his measly hands over his chest and looked like he was going to cry. "And I want my dad's army stuff back."

"One of these days, I'mmona fuck you up, Gareth." Aidon plowed away from the curb and watched in the mirror how snowy slush splattered back onto his cousin's legs.

"Prick!" Gareth yelled, but Aidon didn't care. He was getting everything ready so he could open his present.

He took Pearl to Twenty-sixth, to the drive-through, and ordered himself three double cheeseburgers, some onion rings, and a jumbo Slushee.

"Want anything while I'm here?" he said to his present, but she didn't give him a straight answer, just whined something he couldn't understand. "You don't know what you're missing," he said, and he pulled up and paid for his food. He was even nice to the pimply, chubby fleshpot at the cashier window.

Seventh heaven. Those were the best words he could think of to describe how he was feeling. He pulled into a parking spot in the very corner of the lot. The burgers were hot and salty, and the onion rings were crunchy and sweet, his drink as frosty as it was outdoors. He had all the stuff he needed, and he had something great to look forward to for the first time in a long time. He turned up the heat and the music and smacked his food down. If she didn't want any of what he was having, that was her problem. Nobody could wreck this day.

When he was done, he crumpled up his trash. After he surveilled the lot, he backed up, pulled out onto the road, and turned the wheel toward the nearest gas station. He had to piss like a firehose. He didn't dare risk filling the tank, getting out of the truck right there out in the open with her in there, but he could pull around the back and go in the men's room and drain his own fucking tank. That made him laugh. He edged right up to the bathroom door, hauled out the duffel, took her in with him, and held her up over his shoulder while he whizzed. He could feel how she was shivering, and he wondered if she was going to keep that up and whether that would make it feel even better when they got to the hideout and got down to it. He put her back in the truck and made sure her door was locked, and he looked across Seventeenth, past his old high school. The Flatirons were up there beyond, but he couldn't see them. Still too much snow flying. But the thought of getting up there where they could be together made him smile.

Chapter Twenty-Four

‿

2:00 PM
Sunday, June 20, 2021 | Boulder Mountain Park

Erin had driven a long way into the hills above the Flatirons, along the winding hairpins of Flagstaff Road, searching for an intersection with the closed mining road Tom Drake had mentioned. She'd seen it become winter again and then summer again, hot and dusty and the flicker of the sun spiking through the trees and across the windshield. She was tracking how much time was elapsing, and she'd taken note of the minute when winter ended. She could see now that the intervals were getting shorter. *And in that other frame,* she thought, *he's had her for more than two hours.* A chill of loathing ran down between her shoulder blades. There wasn't a photo of him in the file she'd seen, but after Korrie's funeral there was an image of him on the news, a slightly out-of-focus, closed-circuit photo of him smiling. *Looks happy,* she'd thought, with an alarmingly sharp need to crush that face, to cave in that smile with something heavy and blunt.

And what was the plan now? To meet him head-on? With no way to protect herself? What could she possibly do when she found him? Simply convince him to give her child back to her? Threaten him? Make a bargain? She would have to figure something out when the time came. It was that or give up and go back home.

She followed the double yellow lines along Flagstaff Road, but when she passed the reservoir, she realized she'd gone too far. Flagstaff would twist as far as the campgrounds and back to the highway. She was wasting time. She was making another mistake. She slammed the heel of her palm against the steering wheel. She hated that she was in this bind and didn't know what to do. Her nerves started to rage again. She whipped the car around, veered too close to the fall-off at the far side of the narrow shoulder, and raised a cloud of dust and a spray of gravel. She slammed on the brakes so she wouldn't send the car and herself down the side of the mountain.

"Erin," she said, "cool it." She took a deep breath, nudged the car forward onto the asphalt, and straightened it in the right direction. "There's still time," she reassured herself, and she headed back the way she had come.

She slowed the car in front of the Realization Point trail-head at the entrance to Boulder Mountain Park. This was the third time she had scoured this stretch of the road. It had to be here somewhere. As Erin woke her phone to search the Internet for the closed road, she realized she'd traveled into a cellular dead zone within the park. The indicator read "No Service." But at least the digits still ticked off the seconds on the clock.

She clicked the band of her ring against the smoothness of the steering wheel and searched the side of the road. Brush and rocks, stumps and sand. At last, set back from a gravelly junction, a concrete block sat marked with an aged sign that read "No Entry," and she noticed what was left of a faded road marker. She had to take the chance that this was the old mining roadway. She turned onto the decaying pavement and edged around the concrete block.

The condition of the road forced her to drive slowly. Ruts, cracks, and potholes littered the surface, as if it had been targeted in aerial bombardment—an unmaintained road no one used anymore, exactly as Tom Drake had described. She rolled forward, searching for a sloping trail, the one the skiers had crossed before they found Korrie.

As she drove, she scanned the dense, dry forest around her, everything rocky and arid, and the trees, either still green or red and gray with beetle kill. She opened her window as the car crept along the pitted road. All she saw was the heavy cover of the woods; the only sounds she heard were dog-day cicadas and the clacks and caws of crows.

When an open path of soil appeared at the side of the road, she pulled over and got out. *This could be a trail.* She stepped into the soft soil and followed it for a few dozen yards until she saw that it was only a dry creek bed that dead-ended in a small gully overgrown with clumps of sage. She ran back to the car and headed farther along the road.

As the time approached when she expected the interval to change again, she was on the verge of heading back along the other side of the road, until she came upon a narrow trail that led into the trees. The trail was well defined and well worn. A short distance down the slope stood a semicircle of ponderosa pine trees. *This must be it.* She dreaded the idea that she might get out and stand in the same place where he had stood, where he had discarded what he stole. But perhaps if she were to stand there in winter before he did, she could find a way to undo what he'd done before he did it.

When she jumped out of the car, she searched the ground nearest to where the trail intersected with the old asphalt. Tracks from the wide tires of mountain bikes snaked along the trail and disappeared down the slope below. Tom had said that the skiers came to the junction where the trail crossed the old road and found Korrie some twenty paces away in a semicircle of ponderosa pines. It must have been such a horror for them to realize what they were seeing.

2:15. Twenty paces. She felt rickety and queasy as she counted twenty paces and headed for the pines, for the spot when time would change.

Chapter
Twenty-Five

❧

2:20 *PM*
*Sunday, June 20, 2021 | National Institute of Standards
and Technology*

In the dimmed room, Zac sat forward into the blue light
from his monitor. He felt as if every muscle fiber in his
body were about to take flight, as if every neuron in his
brain were about to fire. He and the guys had continued to
push through this day, reconfiguring the simulation again
and again, each iteration born of a finer alliance with the
incoming data. And now, because of their certainty that the
black hole had formed, all of the world's observatories would
search for some hint of its rotation, some ultraviolet glow of
its evolution.

He and Mark had validated the data from the wave that
had been recorded at 1:32, and they'd sent the packet to Jin,
who now worked furiously to transform it into the graph-
ics that might depict what they all hoped to see: the thing
that would vindicate their rebellion—not the black hole's

formation of a singularity, but rather its transition into a time-reversed white hole.

Walter heaved out a breath of exasperation. "Jin," he said, "are we ever going to see this? What are you doing?"

"Perhaps a little light redecorating." Jin chuckled, clearly pleased to taunt Walter in the mildest way. "What we really need," he added, "is another time crystal for you. Then we could triangulate you with the sim and the white hole, and you could clock it yourself and stop bothering me."

"Wouldn't that be mind-boggling?" Zac said. Something else occurred to him. "Diamonds have been entangled for quantum computing. Why couldn't we do that? Maybe if two crystals tuned to each other in quantum entanglement shared the same vibrational state over a distance, we could use them to find out what happens to time because of the white hole."

"That's what I was saying this morning," Jin said. "Why does no one recognize my genius?"

"Can we please stop speculating and see what we actually have right now?" Walter said. "All genius aside, we need to get going."

Jin squinted at the information on his monitor and said, "Okay, a five, six, seven, eight . . ."

The four men stood and gathered in a row in front of the big screen. Behind the glass, the perturbed gray sea unfurled and reached toward the horizon. In the center of the image, a smooth black sphere emerged out of the gray, and the gray responded by slowly beginning to stretch into circular bands of reflection around it.

"Lensing," Walter said. "I like it. Very realistic."

"Thank you, kind sir," Jin said, and he returned his attention to the screen. In the far distance, beyond the black hole, two inward-angled waves formed and rose and purpled as the other earlier ones had done, and they hurtled toward their meeting point.

Zac gestured toward the screen and said, "This is where the schemata of the sim will diverge."

"Yep," Walter said, as if he'd already known what Zac wanted to say, though he hadn't previewed the way the sim would section off the two scenes. When Zac paused, Walter said, "Go on—tell me anyway."

So Walter was humoring him, and he chose to humor Walter in return. He pointed toward the split screen. "The lengths of the waves that skate past the photon orbit of the black hole are weakened by its gravity, but they continue onward, so the sim shows the set after they meet and how they form this chessboard interference pattern."

Flat squares on the surface of the gray expanse skirted toward the foreground region of the screen, each square bordered with the rolling fringe of beads, mercury throwing off arcs of blue to white, like lightning, at the intersections.

Walter shook his head. "I still think it's too pretty."

"In fact," Jin said, "this is the scaled-back translation. If we let it, it would be even prettier."

On the screen, as the square waves traveled toward them, the image seemed to slip and skip forward slightly.

"What was that?" Zac turned to Jin. "Did you see that?"

"I saw it," Mark said. "A stutter."

"Yeah." Jin shifted to the other foot. "I don't know."

Mark said, "Could it be the monitor? A lag in the refresh rate?"

"Nope," Jin said. "Shouldn't be."

"That's a little nerve-racking, Jin," Zac said. "Let's run a test on the monitor after this data set."

Walter said, "Maybe it just doesn't appreciate art." He smiled to himself.

Zac called Walter's attention to the other side of the split screen. "But here is what we think happens to the gravitational waves that fall into the black hole." He took a step back and folded his arms. The others realigned with him.

The perspective of the sim behaved as if the viewer were flowing atop a current, surfing a purple wave through the glittering photon sphere and onward over the dark waterfall of the event horizon. The momentum of the wave elongated into a cascade and then prismed into bright strings of color. The brilliancy lasted only for an instant before darkness swallowed the strings and the screen became nearly black, with only the rush of quivering dark helixes corkscrewing inward toward the center. Tiny obsidian beads glinted and ricocheted within each helix. As the rush toward the core accelerated, another dimension formed. While one edge of each helix continued traveling inward, the other edge began to travel backward, and in the middle, the flecks of obsidian split into spinning pairs and whirled away from each other.

The men watched, checking each other's faces like fascinated children. At the core of the black hole, a pinpoint of white appeared. The black helixes smoothed out and stretched toward it, the drag of the rotation pulling them inward in a pattern like the sectioned interior of a black nautilus shell.

Walter said. "Will someone explain how this Hollywood stuff is even relevant?"

"It won't be beautiful," Mark said, "if it has to be explained." He waited for a second, as if Walter might concede, but when he didn't, Mark continued. "Nevertheless, the algorithm makes the visual metaphor. Entropy increases until the temperature shifts at the value of the golden ratio."

Walter tucked up one corner of his mouth. "A nautilus shell doesn't actually follow the golden ratio."

Jin stood taller in defense of his work. "But this black hole will, Walter. If you had the imagination to see it. This is what precedes quantum tunneling. The whole thing we're looking for."

"All right." Walter turned to Jin, with his brows pulled together. "Let's not get bristly. I'm just saying—" He let his complaint fade off as he redirected his focus to the screen.

Zac tried to segue back into the math where Walter felt at ease. "The golden ratio will show when the black hole geometry decays, when quantum tunneling allows the transition to the white hole. Then, within the white hole, time itself will reverse."

The white point became a spinning sphere, and the dozens of surfaces within the shell shape took on the appearance of mirrors, reflecting the point over and over into infinity. The chambers of the shell mirrored each other, brightened, turned inside out, and unspooled in the opposite direction. In a dizzying reverse blast, the mirrors refracted with the color spectrum. The screen illuminated to peak radiance. Then it flooded with white. All movement settled and slowed. The long stretch of the smooth, creamy surface rippled gently into the distant perspective. "The white hole," Mark said, "in all its glory." Tiny fiery particles of light glittered atop the ripples.

"Still with the consciousness there, I guess, huh?" Walter sounded as if he were trying to be accommodating.

Zac nodded. "Everything plays its part." A rich sense of fulfillment came over him. The sim was giving them a preview of what should start to happen in only a few minutes' time, and his system flooded with a pleasurable anticipation. "And eventually, as the time-reversed white hole decays and entropy increases, all of the energy will be expelled into some version of the future."

The luster of the wavelets rising and falling cast a peaceful glow over the room. Walter was silent, head down, blinking with his thoughts. Finally, he said, "This rendering is very artistic. It's a beautiful little story, I grant you that, guys. But how do I use it to get everyone on board?" No one said anything. "Seriously, how do I present this in terms of nuts and bolts? How do I go into a meeting and own this?"

Zac glanced at Mark and shared a moment of understanding with him. Here they stood. With Zac's time crystal and his model, with Mark's technical mastery and Jin's artistry, they had unraveled a great secret of the physical world. Time did not work like a machine any more than consciousness worked like a computer. Time and the mind were like waves and the sea, aspects of each other and inseparable.

"Walter," Mark said, "it doesn't have anything to do with nuts and bolts. You don't have to own it. You simply gaze in wonder with the rest of us."

Chapter Twenty-Six

⌒

2:31 PM
Sunday, June 20, 2021 | Boulder Mountain Park

Erin saw nothing remarkable in either direction, just the wind moving through the fading grass of midsummer, typical mountain brush and rock. She'd stopped at twenty paces down the slope of the trail. To her right stood the half-circle of ponderosa pines. Young trees in pale new plumage, as yet unaffected by beetle kill. She checked her phone. 2:31. She braced herself for the cold, snowy afternoon ahead as she waited through the hot, dry, buzzing seconds until the time shift came.

The world slipped into a winter's twilight. All of a sudden, the day was nearly gone. Erin's mind took a second to catch up. Silvery-gray flakes surrounded her, and the ground was soft beneath the soles of her boots, where she stood in the cushion of a two-foot snowfall. It was dusk. Her heart geared higher.

She'd skipped hours.

The young trees stood in the unbroken stretch of white before her. Somewhere here was the spot where he had left her, would leave her before morning. She looked at the white hollow beneath the ponderosas. A confused rage rose inside her. *How could he do that to her? Do what he did and then leave her out here? And how can this place look so ordinary?* It should have looked like a shrine, but it was as plain as any other patch of snow in these hills.

She pushed her questions aside because now it was up to her to make sure none of that was going to happen. She focused on what she had to do next and scanned the terrain around her. The wind had let up, and the snowfall was diminishing. There were no signs that anyone else had been here, nothing unusual. Except that she'd been thrown back into the past again, but further forward in that past day, somehow.

She looked deep into the woods in the fading light. When she woke her phone, a red warning flashed that the battery was low. Between flashes, the time blinked white on the background image of Korrie's face. 5:32. Moments ago, it had been mid-afternoon. Now suddenly, it was past sundown. How had she jumped so much in time?

The coroner's voice dropped into her mind. At one point in the anarchy of those days after Korrie's death, Rebecca Kincaid had said, "We think he had her ingest them three to four hours prior." Now suddenly it was the window of time when Clype would give Korrie the pills.

Erin refused to let panic take over. She stomped through the drifts of snow to the roadway and stood at the edge. The wide tracks of a truck ran down the middle. Him? Her mind grappled with the thought. Were they from him? Was she in the right place? Maybe, but now she faced a deeper problem with time. The pills.

She turned toward the east because Tom Drake had hypothesized that Korrie's body was placed near the trail as Clype left the abandoned road and headed back toward the major arteries into town. She ran along the wake of the tracks, her boots squeaking against the snow as she shivered in the failing light, and she scanned the hillside on either side of the road. As it grew darker, the hollows between the hills became deeper, and her line of sight became shorter.

Wheezing, she eased up. Her breath floated white in the air and disappeared. Her phone read "No Service" and flashed the red low-battery alert. How far should she follow these tracks, not knowing if they were his? She held her breath, hoping to hear something, anything. It was frightening, the sense of being out here alone, exposed to whatever might wait in all that stillness.

She ran, perhaps a quarter of a mile, until something ahead of her drew her attention. Halfway up one of the hills, a yellow gleam of incandescence stood out sharply through the trees. She ran closer until the light vanished behind the slope of the hills. When she thought she was as near as she could get without passing where she'd seen that yellow glow, she started up the white hillside.

She picked her way through the bare aspens and up the snowy incline. It was hard work climbing the cold upslope through the waves of snow. She was winded when she reached a rise and looked up. Squares of light shone from an old, derelict building shoved up against the rock of the mountain. Could this be something? It was evening. On a closed road. So there were no homes up here. Who would have lights on up here now? She tried harder to keep her steps quiet in the creaking snow as apprehension spidered over her skin. She pressed on until she reached the level ground the building sat on.

There was a pickup truck in front of the structure. With hunter's flashers and a plow. She'd followed this black truck to the school. The jolt made her stagger.

She crept closer and angled toward the back of it. That bumper sticker was plastered on the tailgate. She couldn't read it from where she stood, but she knew what it said because she'd already seen it. That morning, she'd been only a car's length away, only a moment behind. She pressed her hands against her forehead and looked past the truck at the light coming from the windows of the building. *Korrie, Korrie,* she thought, *are you in there?* She took a step forward.

A blast of heat and flame unfolded around her. Thick molten light and black smoke walled her in, howling fire on the wind. All shock and reflex, she turned and ran through the hot gaps between the blazing trees. Choking vapor curled around her face. She gasped for air. Tall flames crackled, and trees exploded in her path, but she kept running. Her eyes burned.

She charged through the flaring grove, down the roiling hillside. The earth loosened beneath her feet, and she slipped down the embankment into the ravine at the side of the old road. She sprang back up and ran.

Massive walls of fire leapt upward on both sides of the road. She raced down the center. Pines erupted into forty-foot torches. Heat baked the air. A burst of embers pelted the road in front of her. She charged forward, the battered asphalt before her blurred by smoke. Flaming branches crashed onto the road. She dodged them, in terror of her clothes catching fire.

A sudden roar of wind shoved her sideways toward the wall of flame, and she staggered back to the center of the road. A tree trunk smashed down beside her like a Roman candle, sparks geysering outward. She swerved around it and raced onward. The wind whipped up a cyclone of flame that whirled around her.

Ahead, a patch of clear light appeared through the smoke. Bonfires of fallen beetle-kill flamed in the middle of the road, and she ran on, clinging to the edge of the shoulder. Gasping, she reached the border where the smoke thinned and the light shone.

When she cleared the darkest of the cindered air, she slowed and wiped her stinging eyes with the sleeve of her hoodie. She breathed the air. Reaching a safe place beyond the fire, under the blue cliff of an afternoon sky, she stopped and looked back at the massive shifting undersea of gray smoke. She couldn't understand how this had happened. Now she had no idea where she was, or rather *when* she was, or what to do, but she knew she had to get back, back to where she'd been, to find out if Korrie was in that building.

PART III

The White Hole

Chapter Twenty-Seven

⌒

3:00 PM
Sunday, June 20, 2021 | National Institute of Standards and Technology

Zac sat at his dock in the motionless, pristine limbo of the Clean Room. While Walter grumbled in front of a monitor, typing, deleting, with noises of discontent apparently designed to draw attention to his effort, Mark and Jin worked on silently, heads squared to their monitors, foreheads tensed with exertion.

Zac replayed again and again the snippets of the sim's stutter. Now that he was looking for them, he'd found more. There were six. Every time they'd reconfigured the simulation, a new one had appeared.

"Hey, Mark," he said, "could you come here?"

Mark scooted around the corner of his dock in his chair, spinning it in a pirouette as he rolled toward Zac. "You rang?"

"I've been looking at these stutter points." He nodded toward the black glass. "And I have a terrible thought."

"Wow, sounds painful." Mark smiled.

"When I built the model," Zac continued, "I structured it so that after each waveform passed, the baseline would return to zero."

"Right." Mark nodded and raised his eyebrows in assent.

"Because all of our instruments return to zero after each wave."

"*Correctamente.*"

"The detectors return to their initial state."

"And so . . ." Mark said, rolling his hands around each other, urging Zac to get to his point.

"But spacetime doesn't."

Mark's eyes shifted downward, and he blinked hard with recalculation.

"It never returns to its original state," Zac continued, "and I think that's where the stutter is coming from. At first, I thought it was screen tearing on the monitor or an error in the sim, but now I think it's the sim just showing us what it sees. I think those stutter points are gaps between where I zeroed out the model and the fact that spacetime never recovers after it's torn by a gravitational wave."

"You're talking about the offset—"

"Exactly," Zac said. "And so I have to strip out the part of the formula that brings the sim back to zero." He began calculating the string of code he would need.

Mark said, "Damn." He pushed back from Zac's dock. "I see what you're saying."

"Jin," Zac said, typing faster now. "Can you join?"

From his dock, Jin looked up and said, "What are you kids doing? Did you break it?"

Mark, straight-faced, said, "We need you in here now."

"Shit." Jin grinned. "You did. You broke the universe. I'm telling Mom." When he still couldn't get a laugh, he said, "What, guys?"

"Could you please join on Zac's?" Mark said, and Jin scooted in to his keyboard and punched in his string of keystrokes.

Walter rose and hovered behind them.

"Okay, Jin," Zac said. "Could you input this and see what things would look like then?"

"I suppose." Jin's fingers raced over his keyboard as he initiated the command to pull the code back into his application. "Hey, guys," he said as he focused on it, "are you sure you want me to do this?"

"Please," Mark said.

Walter began to pace. "So are we having problems, or are we just looking?"

"Just looking," Mark answered, but he sounded tentative.

Zac could feel the tightness between his ribs as anxiety started to rise in him. He feared that the cause of the stutter was irreconcilable with the facts of existence as they knew them—that the sim was pointing out a flaw in their knowledge. *We have no idea,* he thought, *what becomes of the time that is torn.*

"One more sec." Jin let out the soft warble of a bird whistle. "Almost rendered." He hit a single stroke on his keyboard. "Minkowski," he said. "I'm sending it now."

The four men returned to the large monitor, and a moment later the pale froth of the unperturbed sim stretched out before them. A wave rose in the background, bled into purple, formed a beaded peak, and advanced toward them.

"So far, so good," Walter said.

The wave reared to its greatest height, crested, and washed over the screen, and there, behind it, formed a black gap in the perturbed region of spacetime, and the interior walls of the gap were mirrored. Within their reflections, tiny beads of light plinked against the walls as if they were fighting to escape. After a second, the mottled gray force of the surface rushed over the gap, and it was gone.

"What the hell?" Walter said. "What did you do to the sim?"

Zac realized he wasn't breathing and drew air into his stagnant lungs. "We made it true," he said. "True to life."

"Explain whatever that was." Walter's face turned hard and white as a turnip.

Zac felt cornered. He said, "We stripped out the assumption that the disrupted time returns to its previous state. Because it doesn't."

Mark intervened, enunciating the revelation as it was dawning on him. "I think this is the way the sim registers loss. I think it's trying to show us that the time that is ripped apart by the gravitational wave is permanently lost. What once existed is—obliterated."

It occurred to Zac that there was something about this that made sense, something recognizable. He thought about when he was a kid at the beach, how he'd tried to understand the way the newer waves crashed over the fading wash of the older waves and erased them, how he used to build towns at the edge of the water on Black Sands Beach and watch the waves wash them away. When he was at Berkeley, he'd once written Erin's name there. He remembered the time he'd nearly drowned when he was pulled beneath the surface and away from shore by the rip current.

The stiffness of Walter's expression remained. "That's not possible though."

"I know," Zac said. "That was my first thought."

"Time can't be destroyed," Walter stated. "All of its quantum detail is perpetual. It can't just be deleted from the cosmos." He faced Mark. "But . . . you're saying it will be."

"Yes." Mark answered.

"Go back, Jin," Walter said. "Run that part again."

Jin set the sim on a loop to show the rise of the wave, the crest, the appearance of the black gap and the beads of consciousness trying to break out, and then the flood of gray as it vanished.

"This is a disaster," Walter said. There was a long minute of resigned silence from all four of them. Then Walter looked at them and said, "You're sure about what we're seeing?"

Mark, Jin, and Zac, all three of them sobered now and grim, nodded yes as the sim replayed.

Zac mulled the implications he couldn't put into words. Something about the stitched nature of lifetimes, fragments of human lives, splices ripped away without anyone ever knowing it.

"If this is true . . ." Walter said, "I'll have to think about how to bring it to Schacht." He shook his head, and his shoulders drooped in a posture of defeat. "This is not what she was expecting to hear from us." He put his hands in the pockets of his coveralls and lowered his head. When he looked up, he said, "And this will look like shit in a press release."

"Unparalleled shit," Zac said.

Jin reset the graphic loop. Then, as it replayed in slow motion, he extended his hands in the sweep of an imaginary headline. *"Universe Edits Human Existence—All Advised to Take Longer Vacations."* He chuckled to himself, and the others contemplated silently as the gap appeared, the mirrored interior revealing the frenzied urgency of the mercurial beads, until it all disappeared beneath the gray.

Chapter Twenty-Eight

❧

5:30 PM
Sunday, June 20, 2021 | Boulder Mountain Park

Erin stormed back and forth across the cracked road a short distance beyond the leading wall of the fire. Why? Why was this happening? The fire kept her from where she had to go. She had tried to hike around it to get back to that building, but the surge ripped through the dull grass and beetle-killed trees and up the lichened rocks in a hiss of crackling vermillion. It was spreading so fast that it had driven her back to the road. Shreds of flame leaped up and disappeared black into the umber clouds of smoke. The wind had a sweet and fiery itch, and her eyes stung. Sparks skittered toward her and glowed in the seams of the pavement.

Her veins thumped with desperation to find a way to get through the fire, to get back to that building and find out if Korrie was inside.

That truck. The driver who'd leaned over to look at the children. If she had known then.

She woke her phone again. It was 5:30 now, but she had already reached 5:30 before, when she was in winter. She wondered how much later it would be with the next shift. The only thing that seemed predictable was that it would happen at thirty-two minutes after the hour, whatever hour she would be thrown into. She was going to have to conserve what little battery power she had left. It was draining away, even though she had no service.

As the hot wind changed direction, sirens keened from a distance behind her. She turned and looked down the unburnt road. Fire trucks? Her first impulse was to run to meet them. But what could she tell the firefighters? That she needed them to create a firebreak so she could climb that slope, get back into the center of the blaze, back to the building at the heart of it? No. If a fire crew found her here, they would probably make her leave the area, set her back even farther from where she needed to be. Either in this time frame or the other, she had to get back to where she'd seen the black truck. She crept closer to the yellow surge of fire billowing across the paving. The air crackled around her. She pleaded for it to happen, the shift. *Send me back,* she thought. *Let me find out.* The sirens quieted and then grew louder again with the curves of the road, and she approached the pulsing diagonal wall of fire that blocked the way back.

"Now," she said. "Please now." The intensity of the heat drove into her skin. "Please."

And instantly she inhaled the frozen atmosphere of a winter's late afternoon. Feathery flakes gusted around her in the wind. She zipped her hoodie up to her neck and scanned the frozen road. The tire tracks were sharper now, fresher. She ran in their wake, pulling her phone from her pocket. 4:32.

It was shifting earlier, not later? The sequence of the intervals had reversed? Why? And if so, how much time did she have?

She searched for the hill where she'd seen that incandescent light. There was no glow to head for; there were no footprints from her trek earlier. *Or was that later?* She followed the tire tracks a long way until they turned where another road forked up the hillside. A wide depression in the snow showed the moment when the vehicle had pushed a plow up the road earlier in the storm. The truck. At the junction sagged a worn metal sign: "Three Dog Knight Mining Mill Co."

The first thing that swept into her mind was *ore dust.* The autopsy report had indicated patches of ore dust on Korrie's skin.

Furious energy flashed down Erin's legs. She ran up the plowed trail.

The shape of the building emerged from the snow. There it was—the slight radiation of yellow from the windows, the black silhouette of the truck. She'd found it. She scanned her surroundings. No one. No movement.

One boot in front of the other, she advanced forward, each footfall too loud. She wanted to rush to the windows, but she slowed herself. She approached the truck, heavy-duty, the plow, the hunters' flashers, the bumper sticker on the back. Unbelievable. The same one. All of her awareness heightened, she peered through the driver's window. Nothing but some trash on the seat.

Beyond the truck, the windows of the building were opaque with condensation. She would have to get closer to see anything. As quietly as she could, she rounded the front of the truck and stepped across a depression where drifting snow had settled into a line of large footprints leading toward the door. Old planking skirted the front of the building, and she tested it before she stepped up onto it, then crouched close to the first window frame.

Holding her breath, she inched toward the clear center of the pane. She peered inside. Was he in there? Would it be him? The smiling face? At the far end of the room, indistinct old equipment sat piled in dusty decay. As she leaned farther for a better look, an old cabinet cleared the frame, the hot orange pulse of filaments in a space heater, the star-shaped light coming off a low-hanging bulb.

Then she saw Korrie. Erin's heart bucked against her ribs. Her vision flashed blank for a second. She clapped a hand over her mouth, silencing the shock.

Korrie. Alive. She sat in her underwear on the surface of a desk, her hands behind her back. Sitting in the chair in front of her was that man. Clype. He gawked up at her face. He had his hands on her bare legs.

Shafts of terrible anger shot through Erin. She strangled the need to yell. Her body wanted to launch into the room. Both hands over her mouth, she made herself stay mute. *Do something.* Thoughts jammed themselves in front of each other. *Do something. Do something!*

With the effort to stand, she slipped on the icy plank and thumped her forehead on the edge of the window frame. Clype's head whipped around.

She ducked backward and held her breath, waiting to see if he was coming, if she would have to face him.

Chapter
Twenty-Nine

～

3:44 PM
Sunday, June 20, 2021 | Three Dog Knight Mining Mill

Incendiary heat exploded and sucked the air from Erin's lungs. Flames burst over her, and the blazing building howled. She shielded her eyes and ran, expecting to encounter the same firestorm as before, yet she cleared the fire in a matter of only seconds. It was so much smaller now. She realized the pattern of the reversed sequence was continuing. Out in the open air, she scoped the extent of the fire and then turned and faced the burning building and the ferocity of the heat. Swirls of orange flame leapt up into bright scraps and dissolved into smoke. She hadn't had to face Clype, but now Korrie was left there with him. The flaring sea of red and yellow plumes devoured the grasses and the planking where she'd just crouched, no more than fifteen feet away from her child. She wanted to shout Korrie's name until the world complied and brought her out.

But she's not here now, she told herself. *She's in winter.*

Alive.

There was a chance. There was hope. She battled the furor inside her. Korrie's head had been bent forward so Erin hadn't been able to see her face, only her profile, her hair draped over her shoulder and the slope of her back. Her Korrie.

Erin needed to put her arms around her, to shield Korrie from that monster, and the need was overpowering. She had to get back into this building. A bulge of fire swelled toward her from the front of the structure. Disoriented, reeling, she looked at her phone to try to center herself. June 20. 3:44. Time intervals in reverse order. She had clocked herself at 5:30, at 4:30, and now 3:44. But also shrinking time. Each interval shorter. So a longer stretch before she could see her again and less time when she did.

Have to get back to her. Have to be ready. Find some way to get close to her, get her out of there.

Erin took off amid the smoke and blowing dust, rounded the corner of the building. Back windows? No windows. Only the unbroken walls of the structure. Farther on, though, a door at the very back. She ran to it and yanked on it. Unlocked, but stuck. She pulled with her full weight until it gave, and she stumbled backward. She scrambled into the doorway. Inside was a small vestibule. Empty. Another door on the opposite side of the square room. She took a step inward. From the crack under the opposite door, brown smoke pushed its way in. How long would she have to wait for the shift?

A single pin of fire licked upward. Then, spreading toward her, a thousand flecks of dust ignited along the pine planks like a rush of miniature fireworks. Ore dust. The air in the room seemed to suck inward, and Erin turned and threw herself back outside into the open light. With a loud *whomp*, the doorway filled with roiling gold flame. The percussion caught her and shoved her off her feet. She picked herself up and backed away. The grass at the foot of the doorway crackled with fire, shriveling and blackening toward her.

She rushed around to the front of the building, searching again for a way to hide herself until she could see how to get to Korrie and then get her out safely. As she faced the burning frame, the wind came from behind her and whipped flames and sparks upward in a funnel, and then the current changed direction and blew burning cinders toward her.

She backpedaled, and her boot came down on something that gave with a snap, like cardboard breaking. She looked down. A box of *her* matches. She stooped and picked them up. The last box of the special ones. She reached into her pocket. The matches she'd put there were gone. Her mind stumbled. How could her matches be here?

On the ground in the blackened area stood a pyramid of short branches, carbonized, still smoking. They were arranged the way she'd laid a fire when they used to go camping. *And* my *matches*. How was this possible? It was as if she had started this fire, but she didn't remember doing it. Had she set the blaze that was destroying the place where she'd seen Korrie?

"I have no memory of this," she said aloud.

Why would she have done it? She examined the matches again. Their three faces looking out from the front of the box. She paced the outline of the growing fire front, and the wind sent another shower of sparks raining down from the heart of the blaze. A sense of déjà vu flashed in her mind, as if she'd stood in this spot and asked questions before, but then, just as quickly, it was gone.

She had come all this way, through each of these mystifying shifts. She had found this place and she had found Korrie. She was in position now, ready to do whatever she had to do to take back her daughter when the interval shifted. But now it seemed she had taken another step at some point she couldn't recall, the destructive step of setting fire to this building.

"Erin, what did you do?" she whispered.

Chapter Thirty

3:44 PM
Sunday, June 20, 2021 | National Institute of Standards and Technology

Zac needed his old notebook. He wanted to look back and remind himself of his thinking from when he'd first visualized the math. Maybe if he could see his handwritten notes, sketches for the sculpture of his original model, he could discover something he'd missed. He'd wracked his mind and come up empty-handed in the search for anything that would miraculously heal the rip in the sim, anything that could prove his math wrong and show conservation of the wholeness of time. But his notebook was in a drawer in his office.

And he needed to talk to Erin. He felt stripped of the scaffolding that held him up, and he wanted to hear her voice, feel the old certainty of the good years they'd had together, the comfort of the one person who knew him through and through. Where could he find her again, that woman he was remembering?

"I'll be right back," he said.

All three men wheeled toward him as if he'd set off a firecracker. "Where are you going?" Mark asked.

"Just to my office," Zac said. "I'll be back in one minute."

"Are you kidding?" Jin said, his expression dead-flat serious.

"Don't panic, guys," Zac said. "I swear I'll be back in a minute. I need my notebook." He slipped through the glass doors before anyone—Walter—could object. Once he began to peel off his coveralls, it was easier to breathe.

Outside, the air was hot, and it smelled of pine and earth and dust. As he jogged toward the office building, he glanced up at the Flatirons, red and clear and seemingly so close that he felt as if he could just walk home. With a longing that gripped him hard behind his ribs, he wished he could go there. Go back home. He let the smells of the house rise from the depths of memory, some mixture of clove and brown sugar and melted butter. Erin in front of the oven. Erin of old. The girl with heatproof hands. Old-fashioned enough to wear aprons, but the white aprons of elite chefs. A sixth sense about taste and ecstasy. Every little thing a delicious invention. Intricate weavings—braids almost—of flavors. Delighted by her own presentation. And now she was up there, in those hills they'd hiked a thousand times together, in the home they'd put together to please each other, where they'd once conceived a hypervelocity star. Up there still. Starving.

Inside the research building, he opened the door to his office and hurried over to his desk. He unlocked the drawers and reached into the second drawer down, pulled out his notebook, and tucked it under his arm. He opened the top drawer and took out his phone. When it illuminated, the phone icon lit with the red dot of a new voicemail. He pressed the square to take a look and saw it was from Erin. Her picture looked out at him from the small screen, and he tried to remember when she'd looked like that, unburdened, the girl with a thousand expressions, who loved surprises, who lived for delight; how delighted she'd been all those years ago with the ring, with his time crystal; and how she guarded it, even now that the marriage was in ruins.

With a tap, he selected her call. The strange thing was that the voicemail had nothing attached to it. Nothing recorded. So strange. Why would she call and not leave a message? He'd asked her to.

The voicemail had a time stamp of 10:42, but the log read that it was from February 7, 2020. Not today, but February 7, last year. Which was the day Korrie died. Which was impossible.

He called Erin's number, but it went straight to her voicemail.

"Erin," he said. And then he couldn't say anything. Tension tightened within his throat, and he struggled against his loneliness for her. He swallowed hard and said, "Did you call me? Please call and leave me a message."

When he returned, he stopped outside the entrance to the Clean Room and flipped the switch on the intercom. "Mark?" He peered through the glass, and Mark looked up at him. "Could I have a second?" he said. The heads of his friends swiveled as they checked in with one another.

"Sure," Mark said. He got up and came through the doors. "What's up?"

"I want to show you something." Making the effort to slow his breathing, Zac held out his phone, opened to the empty voicemail.

Mark examined it for a moment. "Oh," he said. His eyes rose to meet Zac's. "The date."

"Right," Zac said. "I talked to Erin this morning, and then this came in just a few minutes ago."

Mark looked at the display again. "With the wrong date? And isn't that about the date . . ."

"The exact date."

A twinge narrowed Mark's eyes and then faded. "Did you try her?"

"Went to voicemail."

"Weird," Mark said. "Bad retrieval?"

"No, I don't think it's that." Zac met Mark's gaze, and he could see him rolling the situation over in his mind like a kid who'd found a peculiar rock. Zac hoped hard that some sensible solution would occur to him.

"I can't see how all this"—Mark waved a hand toward the Clean Room—"would have any bearing. I'd call customer support tomorrow," he said. "That's uncanny." He gave Zac a brief smile of apology.

Zac took the phone back. Not what he'd hoped for. "Yeah, I'll do that." And to let him off the hook, he added, "Thanks."

Mark shucked off his coveralls and patted Zac's arm. "You're okay?"

"Yeah," Zac said, despite his pulse chattering faster.

"We better get back to it." Mark stepped into fresh coveralls.

"Right," Zac said. "I just need a minute."

After the doors slid shut behind Mark, Zac decided to make a quick call to his brother. Next level up of people he trusted.

Dan had been the one who, in the days before the funeral, had been responsible for phoning the part of the list that included Korrie's classmates. Zac had been able to hear him, his whispers carrying from the other room. *Hello, this is Dan Fullarton, Korrie's uncle . . .* followed by the inevitable moment, and then Dan's reply. *Thank you,* and *I know. It is hard to imagine.* He would go on to give information about the date, time, and place of the funeral, the burial, and the reception.

During one call, he leaned into the room where everyone else sat. He put his phone against his chest and whispered, "Zac?" When Zac looked up, he saw the loss on Dan's face. Redness, furrows, exhaustion. "This guy, Brennay's father," Dan whispered, "wants to know what he should tell her." Zac looked around the room for help. He sought someone else to give an answer. He looked at Erin, her parents, his parents, Maggie. They all had the same look on their faces, the mystification a child feels when asked an impossible question. It was a room full of kids faced with a task meant for priests.

Today, when Dan finally answered, his hello sounded surprised, excited. "What's up?" he said.

"I need a favor." Zac kept his head and his voice low.

"Sure," Dan said. "Everything okay?"

"Yep," he said, "but I'm locked in here."

"Today's your day, right? Your sim and everything? How's that going?"

"It's . . . interesting." Zac hurried on, "But listen, I got a weird voicemail from Erin."

"Oh," Dan said, his tone one of recognition. The ongoingness of it.

"Well, actually," Zac added, "just a voicemail with no content." He couldn't bring himself to tell his brother about the date stamp in the log.

"Uh-huh," Dan said. "Strange."

"I think . . ." Zac's voice broke. He wanted to collapse into the arms of the boy his brother had once been and cry the way he had when his bearded dragon died. "Maybe there's a problem with her phone or something. I don't know. I would really appreciate it if you could swing by the house and see if . . . and just say hi. Make sure she's okay."

"No problem," Dan said. "I can run up there in a bit, after work."

"Great."

"Around six okay?" His concern softened the timbre of his voice.

"Six," Zac said. It would be a long time until then, and he wished he could get some reassurance right now. "Sure. Thanks. Let me know, okay?"

"Of course," Dan said. "Anything you need."

When Zac hung up, he was powerfully tempted to put his phone in the pocket of his coveralls. He wanted to hold it next to him, but he couldn't take it back into the Clean Room and violate the sanctum that way. The protocol was to lock it in one of the property lockers in the bank of small doors against the wall. Instead, he left it powered on and stowed it above the lockers, propped up against the wall. Tilting his head to test the sightline, he made sure he could see the phone from his dock when a call lit it up. As he checked, Mark watched from inside the Clean Room, and with a nod he let Zac know he understood.

After Zac pulled on another set of coveralls, he took his notebook and reentered the Clean Room. Jin arched his eyebrows and shrugged with a shake of the head as if to inquire wordlessly about what was with all of the secret comings and goings. Zac tried to offer a look of reassurance but it seemed to fail, an unconvincing combination of false fortitude and doubt.

He turned his mind back to the sound of Erin's voice when he'd last spoken to her. That bell-like quality that meant she understood what he was trying to do. He tried to calm himself, but when he sat down to work, his focus was scattered, his thoughts like arrows fired but then lost.

Chapter Thirty-One

❧

The Day Of: Friday, February 7, 2020 | Chautauqua Park

Later in the afternoon, Aidon decided it was time to take her where they could have a little face-to-face time. He took Flagstaff west and drove up into the hills and over to the road to the hideout. It wasn't really a hideout; it was just the mill of the old Three Dog Knight Mine beyond Woods Quarry. According to his uncle, there was still a lawsuit going on from years ago, when fucking inspectors had shut down the mine, but the power was still on to run the venting. Some asshole showed up every now and then to switch it on for a few hours so the whole fucking thing wouldn't go up in a giant fireball. Aidon stayed in the mill sometimes when he had no place to sleep, if his roommate was being a bitchhole about the money or some other bullshit. Never had brought one of his girlies up here, though. Should have thought of this place a long time ago.

It was getting late, like 4:00, when he ran his plow up the slope in front of the mill, and once he'd made sure there was no one else around, he parked and gave the windows at the front of the building a look-see. All nice and dark and quiet, so he could be alone with his present.

When he opened his door, the wind snagged it and yanked it wide, with a blast of snow in his face. He got out and stomped through the snow pile to the passenger side, opened the door, and lifted the duffel with her in it. Light and easy. She slithered some when he threw her over his shoulder, so he smacked her on the ass and said, "Cool it, babe." And she did. He stuffed the pills in his pocket, grabbed the drinks off the seat, and kicked the door shut with his foot.

He got his present inside, but it was fucking cold in there. He put her down on the desk and toed the switch on the space heater. After he flipped all the wall switches, he counted only three bulbs that were working. But that was fine, better for the mood.

He sat his pretty up on the desk and tugged the duffel out from under her and off over her head. He smoothed her hair and took a good look at her face. Holy fucking shit, she was beautiful. The most beautiful one yet.

"Be good, babe," he told her.

He started to tug at the top button of her sweater, a little pearly one. *Lock the door this time, Aidon.* He had to remind himself of some things. He stepped over to the door, spied through the glass to be sure, and clicked the deadbolt.

When he turned back around, she was trying to sneak out the other door at the back of the room. He barreled across the space and grabbed her just in time. Pulled her hair. He didn't mean to do that, but she could have gotten away. Clean fucking away. Little bitch. He pulled her arms behind her back and clamped her wrists in his fist, real tight. He knew he had some big double-tie wraps in the truck, cool ones he'd saved because they were like handcuffs.

He unlocked the door and dragged her out there into the storm. Fuck, what a noise she made. He told her to shut the fuck up and fished around in the back of the cab, with one hand, until he found the tie wraps. Once he got her back inside and got them on her, he held her chin tight and said, "No fucking running." She was still shaking, and her eyes dripped some, but he could fix that. It was going to be a great night.

He took a pull off the Jack and it made him feel warm and romantic. He put the bottle to her lips and tipped it up for her, but she coughed it all out like she had fucking pneumonia or something.

"It's just a little medicine, sweetheart," he told her, and he took another pull. He didn't want to hog it all. "Come on, babe, have a sip." He held the bottle to her lips, but she squinched her eyes and shook her head no. "It'll be easier on you," he said, "if you do what I say." He jiggled the neck of the bottle between her lips and poured in a good chug.

She coughed it up again all over her pants.

"Well, shit," he said, "I'm not gonna give you any more if you're gonna waste it."

He sat back with the Jack bottle against his belly and told her the story about the time he slurped a fifth of Jack or two and snorted some fucking unreal crystal and drove down to Gunnison for a hunting rally with some buddies of his, and how they stayed out in the blind, slurping for two days, and how he brought down a monarch bull, eight fucking points. Which wasn't quite true. He kind of admitted that. But he told her what a great time they had. She was a really good listener.

The bottle was almost half empty by then. He had a nice buzz going, and he thought it would probably be best to get things going soon. She was little and she would probably get tired early. He didn't want to rush. He wanted it to last and last, this time.

"Maybe someday," he said, "we could take a trip to Billings." He popped an oxy out of the pack, pulled out his Army knife, and crushed the red pill into a Pepto-pink powder. "I got a buddy up there with a cabin right on the river." He rolled up a dollar bill and railed the first quarter dose. "Have you ever been fishing?"

She said nothing, but she looked back at him with those beautiful eyes, minky eyelashes, so maybe she needed a second to think about it. The sugary sunrise of the oxy brightened in his head. His whole body rushed with warm goosebumps.

"I fucking love fishing. I could show you."

He sniffed up a second quarter, and within moments, the brightness brimmed golden out beyond his head, smooth and slow and wide. He had a vision of her swimming along in the calm river, naked, lazy, the pale ripply sun diamonding her ass skin as she frog-kicked her legs open and closed. He could tell everybody she was his niece. He wondered if she would think he was good-looking in his swim trunks. Probably another thing that made him attractive to her was how good he was at conversation. He had tons of good stories. Funny ones.

He gently snuffled the third quarter, and then he ran his gaze over her. She was glorious. His mind floated on a shimmery lake of warm light, and he felt like a liquid quicksilver man among mud men. He zoomed in on her pretty cloud-colored eyes.

She said something to him in an airy murmur.

"What was that?" he said and inched closer.

She whispered, "Please let me go."

He sat back. Disappointing. A little dark spot of pissed off. "You're gonna have to relax," he said.

He offered her the rolled-up bill, but she just looked at it. *Of course, stupid. She has no hands.* He popped three pills out of the pack. One little piggy, two little piggies, third little piggy is a charm.

He told her, "This should make you feel great. Super great." With tender fingers, he nudged the pills between her lips and tipped the rim of the cherry Coke bottle for her to slurp. She clamped her mouth shut and made him spill some. "Don't fuck with me!" he shouted. Her shoulders tightened up, and she tensed even more. *Fuck.* He didn't mean to yell at her. "Please," he said, and he gave her his warmest sunbeam-breaking-through-the-clouds smile. "Swallow." He poured a nice blast of cherry Coke between her lips. And she did swallow like a good girl. "Let me see," he said. He pulled her chin down and looked for the red pills. There was still one in there, so he gave her another glug and inspected in there again. All gone. "That's right," he told her. "Nice and simple."

She was only a little wisp of a thing, so he took it easy unbuttoning her sweater. And he slowly and calmly put her over his shoulder to take down her pants. He tugged them to her ankles and then sat her ever so softly back on the top of the desk. After he pulled the pants off over her feet, he peeled off her socks and took a second to admire the glittery purple nail polish on her toenails. Very fancy and elegant. She was the best thing that had ever happened to him so far.

He poured some cherry Coke into the Jack bottle and sloshed it a bit. He wanted to have sweet breath for her, so he chugged a little and let the foam fizzle around his tongue. He scooted in close and put an arm around her, and he pressed his cheek against her perfect pink skin. The smell of her was like fruity candy. And she felt very warm.

His eyes not quite able to focus on hers, he said, "Is it too hot in here?" He thought maybe the space heater was up too high, but he felt fine—amazing, in fact.

A sound startled him. Nearly split him out of his skin. *What the fuck?* Came from outside. Was somebody out there? He hotfooted it over to the door. Damn, he didn't have his rifle with him. If he'd known what was going to happen today, he would have brought it, but it was at home. He unlocked the door and jerked it open. He leaned out and searched both ways. The storm was thicker now, the hills blurry, but he could see pretty far. There was nothing moving out there. *Maybe snow falling off the roof?* He listened for a second. *Nada.* Relieved, he closed the door hard, gave it an extra push shut, and turned the deadbolt. Gave the knob a tug. It was locked for sure. He was safe.

He turned and took in another delicious eyeful of his beautiful girlie. She beheld him with the sparkling-wet eyes of love. It was almost embarrassing to see what a crush she had on him. His blood was rushing hard. It was time now. Time to have his present.

Chapter Thirty-Two

❧

Winter returned with a blast of bitterness and high wind, forcing frost into Erin's eyes. She shivered in the bright, seething chaos of the blizzard, the gray daylight brighter again than it had been before. Still reversed time. But there was no truck—there were no tracks, no prints, not even a hint that Erin or anyone else had already been here. She'd seen the truck—it had been right here. She'd seen Korrie—her baby, alive. But now, nothing. Could her whole plan be ruined? Snowdrifts angled upward, climbing the sides of the building. It could not be true that the right moment had slipped away again. She drove her trembling legs through the deep, cold drifts to the apron of the building and then up to the windows. There were no lights, only the vague shapes of machinery and office equipment in the dimness. No signs of anyone inside.

She stepped over to the heavy metal door. The frozen knob stung the tender pink skin of her palm. She grabbed hold with both hands and pushed hard. The door swung open, and she staggered into the unlit room.

In front of her stood the desk Korrie had been sitting on and the chair that man had occupied. They weren't here. The weight of the emptiness felt crushing. The feeling of having Korrie back in her arms again was now out of reach. The sight of her inquisitive eyes, the sound of her harmonica laugh, the sweet-cream smell of her skin—all beyond Erin's reach now.

But I have to have my daughter back, she thought. Never mind the people who had searched for Korrie; the dogs baying; the whole frantic machine of the missing-person protocol put into motion; the fragile little shape draped in paraffin skin on the coroner's table; the stiff, surreal funeral; the frozen crackling of the brown grass underfoot at Green Mountain; all the months of trying to wake up from real life—all of that could be forgotten if the universe would just give Korrie back to her.

The desk, the chair, and the equipment at the other end of the room were all covered with dust. Crushed beer cans and empty liquor bottles spilled from a knocked-over trash can. They, too, were mossed a dusty gray.

She went to the back of the room, to the door of that vestibule. The small room that had sparked to combustion a few minutes ago was untouched now too. She crossed it to the outer door, pushed hard until it opened, and leaned out into the churning wind. The stretch of snow around the building was unmarked.

She shut the door and closed her eyes. Korrie had been right here in this place. But now no one had been here. She must be too early now. Her phone read 3:35. Where did he have Korrie now? How could Erin find her as she herself was slipping farther into earlier hours of this day? What could she do? She had to come up with another idea.

"Think, Erin, think it out," she said aloud. She turned to the front room of the mill. What did she know about this phenomenon? So little. Only scraps she remembered of the details Zac had spoken about. She and Zac had different kinds of intellect. He was a planner, a man who projected himself into the territory ahead and created strategies. She was a perceiver. She observed the landscape as it unfolded; and as it presented itself, she responded—improvisation. It was the same way she cooked: following her intuition. It was the way she'd raised Korrie: finding her way by instinct. Except for once.

Erin's mind did not retain the physics formulae Zac talked about, but she did remember things that had a story. Months after everything that happened, Zac had told her about a dream he'd had while he was in flight back from India on the day of Korrie's abduction.

In the dream, he was in a restaurant with the team from Hingoli. Some of the Indigo physicists were joking with Zac about his being afraid to fly.

Zac said, "I'm not afraid to fly. Why do you say that?"

One of the scientists said something like "When the god of birds, Garuda, flaps his wings, he can stop the spinning of heaven, earth, and hell." But he was irreverent and entirely secular, and he was mocking Zac somehow.

Then, in the dream, Zac was aboard the plane home, and a shadow crossed outside his tiny window. He glanced out beyond the wing of the plane and saw a murmuration of starlings, a giant swarm of tiny black birds wheeling in the immaculate sky above the clouds, the shape of the flock taking on the movement of waves in water, then morphing into a jellyfish, a swan, a skull, a heart. But as he watched the acrobatics of the shape, it cohered into the sphere of a black hole. From the plane, he could zoom in and see that the birds were very old, weary, and tattered, and then suddenly young and sleek, then skeletal, then liquid, then carbon.

What it meant, he'd told Erin, was that matter didn't matter. "In the shape of time," he'd said, "it's the interactions between memory and the force of disorder that create what time is for us."

The dream had eventually changed the direction of his research, pushed him toward black holes and white holes, where he could search for the deep reality of time.

Erin tried to find something in that dream that would help her now. The intervals were getting shorter. She looked back out the windows and watched the storm tangle in the wind beyond the glass. Though she didn't have the background to understand what was going on around her—the knowledge Zac had—she did have memories. She was made of memories.

Chapter Thirty-Three

❧

Three Days After The Day Of: Monday, February 10, 2020 |
Boulder Police Department, Public Safety Center

Tom Drake was resettling into the L-shape of his desk and
monitors. When he'd returned from his leave, it felt as if he'd
been gone for years, as if his time on the force was in another
life, but it had been only a short leave of absence, really. And
now he was back, and he clung to the feeling of absolution
he'd been granted. He sympathized with the way everyone
was reacting to him—as if they hardly knew him now. Even
Nate, his once best friend, spoke to him as if they didn't have
years of history together. It would take more time, Tom supposed, to regain his faith. But the most important thing was
to be able to manage the work. To be worthy of the endeavor.
To be a competent vessel on this pure white day.

He aimed his mind at his monitors. He was logged in,
and Vigilant was running the plate of a truck. Once the
search-and-rescue dogs had alerted at the rear door of the

school building, the unit had requested all of the surveillance. Then, after the recovery of the child's remains, Tom had requested to be assigned to her case, and today Supe had finally given him the task, and he'd started inspecting the video images. It was this truck that stood out.

The video showed that on the day of the abduction, this vehicle pulled up over the curb immediately adjacent to the school building's rear door. The timestamp was 11:53:50 AM. The driver got out, exited the frame of the video, and several minutes later he returned and got back in.

The camera was mounted at the northwest corner of the building, to cover both the lot and the gate to the playground. The school's entry had an architectural overhang that obscured the passenger side of the truck and the school door itself, but the front license plate was clear, even in the height of the storm.

Tom accessed the DMV data, but the associated phone number was disconnected. The landlord for the registered address reported that the resident had been evicted some months earlier for nonpayment. Tom queried for the license-plate-reader data of that truck for the preceding ninety-six hours and found that it had been all over the city, tracing veins and arteries for hours at a time, in almost constant motion until Friday. Likely the plow, but maybe not just that. He developed a heat map. Lots of repeat visits to public places. Drive-throughs, a convenience store—and schools, a number of schools. Lots of activity until mid-afternoon on Friday, and then nothing. He lengthened the search period a couple days back. Location pins clustered on one hit on successive nights. Likely a different residence.

Two things took up space in his ribcage: the excitement of finding a lead in the case and an interior flittering, an arrhythmia that came and went with a dry, brushing sound that had started its refrain after he'd looked at the little girl's face, sought signs of life and found none.

Even though everyone thought it was ridiculously archaic, he liked to print out his list of hot spots. It would be satisfying to feel the smooth paper between his fingers, and he looked forward to driving to the first location, checking off the hit with a Sharpie, smelling the xylene tang of the ink. And then, if they didn't find the truck's owner there, they would work toward the bottom of the list before end of day, and he would prove to himself that he could fulfill what was asked of him. Something to drive his energy toward evening, toward the solitude of night.

So he walked quickly to the printer, picked up his pages, and folded them into neat quarters that would slide into his pocket. Was Nate keeping an eye on him? Watching his every move because he had previously shown mortal fallibility? Cops instinctively steered away from other cops who showed PTSD symptoms, as if it were contagious. But no, no one was looking in his direction. And when he mentioned a ride to the hot residence of the truck owner, Nate stood immediately and gathered his stuff.

Nate drove and they headed north through Noble Park. He chattered nonstop about getting his Cherokee certified for on-duty use so he could collect a subsidy. He talked about when he and his wife would take the kids to Montana to see their grandparents. He talked about the Broncos. He hardly took a breath. A litany that prevented Tom from adding anything. A good tactic. Let the silt settle.

Nate slowed when they turned off Valmont, and he smiled when Tom pulled out his pages of hot spots. They slowed to a crawl until they turned on Loveland, letting the automatic license-plate reader pick up all the plates in the vicinity. They found the hot address. Tom glanced at Nate, but the tenor of brotherhood was gone, and now there was only observation back and forth between them. They exited their cruiser and looked for the truck, but it wasn't there.

Tom rapped his knuckles against the door of the small residence, and the subject who answered was an emaciated white male in his seventies, wearing a flannel shirt and pajama bottoms. He had no idea of the whereabouts of the owner of the truck in question, a casual renter he had no intention of keeping tabs on. The man's demeanor was forthright, and he assented to a walk-through.

Tom and Nate explored the dingy rooms, heavy with the smells of boiled meat, ripening garbage, and marijuana smoke. They found nothing that merited special attention. They instructed the resident to contact them with any further information. Maybe something would float to the surface. They would have to wait and see.

As they waded through the snow back to their cruiser, Nate said, "Collateral piece of crap, accounted for."

Tom replied, "Primary piece of crap, still unaccounted for."

It was almost like it used to be. And he was confident that he was hiding the physical discomfort in his chest. He held himself upright with good posture, the heft of his vest pulling his shoulders down and back, the cold air making his muscles flex so the tremors wouldn't show. But it was undeniable that something was going on inside his ribcage. That dry flittering, the twitches like a set of tiny claws, the slow clench that left him breathless.

Once he and Nate had settled back into their seats and they'd entered their findings for the hit, Tom pulled out his Sharpie, uncapped it, and checked off the address. The fumes from the black ink filled the car.

As Nate pulled away from the curb, he shook his head and, with a half-smile, said, "Well, at least that hasn't changed."

Chapter
Thirty-Four

❧

Time had pushed Erin even farther backward into the heat and stifling airlessness of the long-shut building. She paced the dry floorboards, dizzy with readjustments—*misoriented* was how Zac would describe it. This was summer. Her own time. Her phone read 3:15. Five hundred days away from Korrie. An hour since she'd last seen her.

Erin looked out the front window of the mill. No fire. A restless, dry wind moved through the grasses at the feet of the unburnt aspen. Shorter shadows, earlier again than before. Sun blared against the dirt around the front of the building. No tracks in the drive. No signs of anyone having been here for a long time. The place was a survey of abandonment. Dust, desertion.

She was trying to reason out a way that this regression could be something other than devastating. If the pattern was that she was going to be pushed only backward, earlier in the day, there was no point in staying here. But if they weren't here in winter, they could be anywhere. And how could she find them now?

She walked again to the door at the back of the room and slowly opened it. The vestibule was empty. She crossed again to the far door that exited the building, opened it, and looked out onto the rocky fall-off. Nothing but decaying equipment, scattered trash, mining tailings piled up against the hillside. All of which would be destroyed in the fire she believed she had set, without knowing why, without remembering doing it, as if some fragment in the sequence had been lost.

She returned to the room at the front of the mill, half-hoping she would see Korrie standing there, ready to be taken home. This was one of the worst of the unknowns about what had happened to her. The investigators had never found this place, had never been able to explain to Erin where he'd taken her, so there was never any context, no way to grasp what had happened, because it was as if it had all taken place somewhere without a location, so not quite within reality. Even when faced with the final conclusion, Erin had felt that if she knew where he'd taken her, it might be possible to settle her mind and start to deal with her thoughts. But maybe that had never been true.

Erin stepped closer to the desk. Dust lay like a white skin on the surface. Absolutely undisturbed. For a second, she felt as if she'd glimpsed this perspective before. Almost without thought, her hand drifted out into the open space where Korrie had been the last time she'd seen her, sitting right here in front of her. The emptiness felt like nothing. She drew her hand back. And there stood the chair where the monster had sat, enthroned.

Under the wheels of the chair lay little wads of something. Erin bent down to look. Dusty little pieces of balled-up pink cloth. She reached for them and picked them up. Recognition. These were the socks Korrie had worn that day. Hatred fired in Erin's throat, corrosive and penetrating. Her jaw tightened and her face flashed hot. She brushed the dust from the socks. Angry tears spilled, and she flicked them away.

Her thoughts fired in quick crosscuts. She'd started a fire here, at some time in the reverse order. Now she wanted to feel the violence of that blaze. She didn't know why the memory was missing, but she had to re-create it now, to burn away every trace of him and the horrific things he did.

As she tucked Korrie's socks into her pocket, she was shocked to find that her matches were there now. This must mean something, and she wanted to understand what it was. Did this moment somehow mirror the memory that was lost? She ran out into the heat of the afternoon and began gathering dry branches. There were many of them, and it didn't take her long to find enough to build a campfire pyramid like the one she'd seen collapsed in carbonized remnants in what, from here, would be the future. She stomped the branches, breaking them into equal lengths, and gathered them together while she searched her memory for the image from the edge of the fire. Where had she placed it in the time that would follow this now? She centered herself in front of the mill's door. Ten paces back. Ten more. This seemed right. She laid the wood down and started to build with three branches in a tripod shape. Next, she added all the others to the pyramid and placed twigs and dry grass under the center. When she was finished, she pulled the matchbook from her pocket, took one last look at the photo, struck a match, and set it in the kindling. As the twigs crackled, she laid the matchbook at her feet, where she would find it later. Because maybe this was important: remaking that memory she'd lost, mending the broken sequence.

Once the fire got started, she snatched one of the flaming branches. She used it as a torch to light the twigs on the other side. They caught, sizzled, fired up, and the campfire hissed to life. It grew upward in a pulsating triangle before her.

The day went suddenly darker. The interval had shifted, and she stood holding her torch in the snowy, sullen cold of nightfall. No campfire. Just the chalk-white layer of snow at her feet. Erin blinked hard because her vision felt strange, as if she were seeing two different distances at once. Only yards before her in the frail dusk sat the truck. The truck was here, and that meant he was here. And beyond the truck, light bled from the windows of the mill. They were here. She felt stunned and relieved and vengeful. And she tried to think fast about what to do.

The cold air stung her eyes, making them water, and when she looked to the side, she was swept with dizziness and disorientation, as if she were looking at her surroundings in the reflection of a curved mirror. She smelled smoke on the wind, not from her torch, but from the other direction. And the dimness of the air was unsettling, as if it had an invisible shimmer in it. Something was off. Corn snow pelted down, more granules than flakes. It caught in her hair and landed on her shoulders. She pulled a grain from her sleeve. When it collapsed between her fingers, it smeared white, like ash.

As Erin approached the truck, she saw that the black paint reflected light that was too bright and the truck was corroded in a way it hadn't been before. She looked up to see what created the reflection, and she saw that the full moon shone smoothly golden despite the muffled ceiling of cloud. Something felt very strange about where she was. She had to control the fear that closed in on her. She had to find a way to draw Clype out of the building so she could get inside, get to Korrie. She needed to create a diversion without him seeing her.

His truck. The place where she'd set the fire when it was summer was near where his truck sat now. She looked at the torch in her hand. Was that it? Was that why she'd started the fire? So she could set fire to his truck?

She plowed forward, off balance because there seemed to be a powerful current of wind along the ground. Couldn't be. Icy grains of snow and an itchy, papery, burning smell blew across her face. Through murky opaline shadows, she crept to the truck and knelt beside the front tire. The skin of the truck's body seemed to blister before her eyes. She thrust her torch under the vehicle. Nothing happened. Snow melted into the knees of her sweats, but she could feel the sharpness of pebbles beneath them. A gust nearly blew out her flame as the wood dwindled. She drew it near her lips and blew until it flared again. She shoved it beneath the undercarriage again, but nothing caught. She swept it back and forth, waiting to see if something would ignite, but nothing did. Soon, the wood burned close to her fingers, and it was getting too hot to hold. She jammed it with all her strength into the metal parts, as far up as she could reach. Sparks pelted her hand, and she pulled it back, making herself keep quiet against the pain.

A smattering of carbonized embers hailed into the snow from the undercarriage of the truck and snuffed out. Maybe this wasn't going to work. Erin stood.

Something else. Try something else.

The ground under her boots crunched like dry tinder instead of the squeak of fresh snow. The mill stood on the other side of the truck, wavering as if it emanated heat. No matter what this strangeness was, she had to keep moving.

She crept toward the door of the mill. The clouded windows obscured her view. What if she could crack the door slightly, enough to see inside? *Have to risk it,* she thought. She reached out and tried the knob. It was warm, as if it had been in someone's pocket. So strange. But locked. She would have to try the other door.

She started to turn away, but just then the door swung open. He stood there. Him. He was framed in rippling light, surprise on his face. Huge, he was. Disheveled. Eyes red. Tiny black pinpoint pupils.

Involuntary stammers escaped her lips. "Hey, I—" she said. "I—my car died . . . and I saw your lights, and I need to use the phone . . ." She heard how false it sounded. "My cell has no service . . ."

From somewhere behind him, Korrie cried, "Mommy!" A piercing, terrified recognition. Erin searched for her beyond him. Korrie screamed again. The man reared up, and like a sledgehammer, his fist clubbed Erin in the chest. In slowed, emulsified time, she felt herself reeling backward. She reached out to catch herself, grabbing the doorframe just as the man flung the door shut. She saw the metal close on her fingers before the pain raced up her arm and splashed over her face. The door ricocheted back open, sparks somehow sifting upward in lazy swirls behind the man.

She pulled her smashed hand to her chest, the pain so enormous it penetrated all the way through her. She looked up at him. "Please let me have her."

With one immense hand, he grabbed her by the front of her shirt, pulled her in, and threw her across the room and into a pile of rusted equipment. A gash of pain tore open along the back of her ribs.

Korrie screamed, "Mommy, Mommy!"

As Erin struggled to rise, he descended on her and stomped on her chest with the sole of his boot. She crashed backward onto a ragged blade of rusted metal, sharp, hot. Pain shot through her. He lurched at her again. She shouted at him, *"Stop!"* He planted his boot on her breastbone and pressed down. Korrie screeched from the corner of the room. Erin saw her in only a sweater and underpants, her hands behind her, tears spilling down her cheeks.

A roar of combustion erupted from outside. Clype jumped back and turned to the windows. In a dark shimmer of air textured like flame, he glowed. With another blast of detonation, a section of a burning bumper crashed through the glass of the mill's windows.

Erin's reflexes raced. She rose, weightless, and tore across the space, scooping Korrie into her arms.

Alive. Alive!

She slammed her way through the vestibule door. The tiny room glittered, haloes echoing around sparks she couldn't see. At the outside door, she grabbed the knob, and her face tightened with the astounding pain of using her wracked hand. She hipped the stuck door open and plunged out into the open air as the room ignited in dark flames behind her.

Pressing Korrie against her bruised chest, she ran. Blind to her surroundings for the moments it took for her to understand that she held her daughter, alive, in her arms. Her legs pumped on autopilot, her mind gauging her ability to outrun him if he followed.

For a second, sirens whined, distant, faint. Her mind clutched at the thought *Rescue us.* But then the sound was gone. The white snow in the trees gleamed opalescent, rainbows of fluxing heat radiation.

The snow-laden space before her cleared to instant black. This was some other place. No, some other time. The air was empty, crystalline, and bitterly cold. Underfoot, the snow was gone, and the ground was completely scorched. The soil crackled beneath her boots, dry and brittle, and before she could judge what was happening, the blackened earth splintered into carbon shards and gave way. She dropped; she let go, and Korrie seemed suspended before her. Then the queasy rush of falling. Her hand shot out to catch Korrie, but she was beyond her grasp.

PART IV

The Labyrinth

Chapter Thirty-Five

～

5:40 PM | Three Dog Knight Mine

They plummeted down a sooty shaft, and Erin tried to grab something to stop the fall. Her hand scraped over dirt, rock, splinters that pierced deep into her skin. She crashed to the floor. Hard earth, dark.

Korrie cried out in pain.

"Korrie," Erin called, nearly blind. "Korrie." She crawled toward the sound of crying, found her. She cradled her child, her Korrie, against her chest. "Are you okay, baby?" She kissed her head.

Korrie sobbed hard, "Yes." She gulped, stuttering with the effort to stop crying. "I'm okay."

Wherever they were, it was so ice-cold it hurt to breathe. Erin pulled herself up onto her throbbing knees and listened for a second to hear if the man was hunting them down, but she heard nothing except the stammer of Korrie's ragged breathing.

She drew the phone from her pocket for light. It awoke, but the screen was laced with fractures, and the light it threw shone only dimly on Korrie's face. Scratches and black streaks of char striped her cheek. Erin laid the phone in the dirt, stripped off her hoodie, and draped it over Korrie's shoulders. She turned her around so she could free her hands, loosen the plastic of the cuff things he'd put on her. Cuffs. Her head swarmed with this reminder of his intent.

"Let's get rid of these." She needed to undo them, but they were clasped tight. She tried to slip Korrie's hands out of the tight bands, but Korrie moaned and Erin quit. She turned her face front and said, "I'm sorry." She zipped up the hoodie, and with a hand on Korrie's shoulder, she said, "You're okay?"

Korrie's breathing hitched and caught in her throat, and she nodded.

"Korrie." Erin reached out and touched her other cheek. Here she was. Her Korrie. Her girl. A mess of joy and terror and relief and fear and pain spun through her.

Korrie shivered. Erin looked into her eyes. "Listen, Squid, I need to know two things," she said. "Did that man touch you?" Her lips were so tense with anger she could hardly get the words out. "Inside your underwear?"

Korrie shook her head.

"Okay," Erin said with a small measure of relief. "Did he give you anything to swallow?"

Korrie's eyes welled wetter and she nodded.

"Pills?" Erin said. "Red pills?"

Korrie nodded. "He made me."

Too late. Erin tried to keep her expression calm, but she was too late. Her eyes burned as the heavy realization sank into her. Too late. "When?"

Korrie dropped her chin and shrugged.

"Can you think back?" Erin held her shoulder. "Was it a little while ago? A long time ago? I have to know."

Korrie's face drew down, and she began to cry again. She shook her head. "I don't know, Mommy." Her frozen breath hung in the air. "A long time ago." She sobbed, "I'm sorry."

Erin wiped tears from the small face and said, "No, Squid. Not your fault. It's going to be okay." In her chest, her heart clenched and wilted, clenched and wilted. "But they're very bad, and we have to get them out of you, okay?"

"Out of me?" Korrie said, her face a small white sculpture of fear.

"I know." Erin stroked Korrie's hair from her eyes with a fingertip. "It'll be okay. Here's what we have to do. We have to make you throw up so the pills will come out, okay?"

Korrie shivered, lowered her head with a soft groan.

"We have to do this, Squid."

Korrie nodded, but distress and cold made her sway slightly from foot to foot.

"Are you ready?" Erin said.

Korrie gave her a quick bob of the head.

"I'm just going to touch the back of your tongue and it'll make you feel sick and you'll throw up those bad pills."

Erin's right hand was swollen, skin tight, red as meat, white stripes across splayed fingers, knuckles like bulbs where the joints disarticulated crookedly. Her left hand was less damaged: blisters, splinters, scratches. Pain lit up, metallic and sharp, as she pried off her ring, with its sharp, protruding diamond, Zac's time stone. She shimmied the ring into her pocket where it would be safe.

With another glance at the ugliness of her hands, she said to Korrie, "Sorry about this." Slowly, with her left hand, she slipped two fingers between Korrie's lips. "Here we go." Korrie's mouth was warm, too warm, feverish. Erin pressed the back of Korrie's tongue until she gagged. She leaned forward and heaved a strangled but empty retch.

"Again," Erin said, and she repeated the effort. She got the same result.

After the third try, Korrie shook her head. Tears flooded from her eyes. She whispered, "I can't do it," and she trembled as if she were about to come apart.

"That's okay," Erin said, and she cradled Korrie's head against her neck. So hot in the icy air. "It's going to be okay." Fleetingly, Erin thought, *My god, you're still six.* The five hundred days had aged Erin by a hundred years, but here was Korrie, still just turned six. "We're going to get you to a doctor, sweetie." Standing up like a scarecrow gathering itself, Erin raised her damaged body. "Let's get out of here."

"Okay," Korrie sniffled.

Erin picked up the phone and swept its light around them. Within a cataract of stone, they stood at the junction of four mining tunnels. Rock walls, ancient beams, trolley tracks leading down into drifts of dirt, dust. No way to climb back up to the shaft they'd fallen through. The phone turned off, saving the last of its power. Erin turned it back on. The shattered display read *5:45 PM, November 1, 2022.* She squinted down in disbelief. How could that be? Now an interval so far in the future? An icon for winter said the temperature was ten degrees.

She had no energy left to dwell in her confusion. Whatever the phone said, she had to get Korrie to the hospital. She had to find her way back to the car. Which tunnel? One led down, the others upward. She chose the one that had a draft, the direction that pressed the chill against her cheeks. Her body cried its pains, but she forcefully ignored it. By some miraculous fluke of physics, the child once taken from her and Zac was theirs again. Breathing, heart beating.

Now she had to find the way to keep her alive. She had to assume Clype could not find them here in this future interval. She had to get Korrie to the emergency room.

She put a hand on Korrie's shivering back and said, "This way, Squid."

Chapter Thirty-Six

⌒

One Week After The Day Of: Friday, February 14, 2020 |
Valentine's Day | Patrol of the University of Colorado campus

Tom was sitting in the warm airflow behind the steering
wheel of his Interceptor, waiting at the snowy corner of Fol-
som and Colorado for the light to change. He'd taken an
extra shift, and it was lunchtime, and he wanted to take a
code seven and go up to the highest seats of the football sta-
dium and see if he could locate himself. For almost a week,
he'd fought hard against this relapse. None of his old tactics
were working, but sometimes the clarity of the air after a
snowstorm helped. He took off his aviators and looked into
the rearview mirror. He had no idea who that was.

On February eighth, for a moment anyway, Tom had
thought he might be okay. When he'd seen Beccs arrive on
the scene that day, the way she'd looked at him, he thought
there might have been something there. Beautiful Beccs. He
saw nitrile gloves on her small hands, long fingers, no ring.

But then the moment passed, and he was alone, with the little bird in his chest.

Now, on the seat next to him lay a shopping bag with a bottle of sun tea, a package of sesame sticks, and a valentine card. He took the card in his trembling hand and looked at the cover. It showed a rabbit holding a hand-drawn heart, offering it to the viewer. It looked kind of stupid to him now. Inside, it read "Hop" and then there was a hand-drawn "e" to spell the word "Hope." "Hope you'll be mine." Was it stupid or not? He couldn't tell what things were anymore.

He drew a pen from his pocket, clicked it to start writing, and reflected on how bad his shakes were now, back again in full force. He flattened the open card against his thigh and wrote, *Dear Beccs, 'Hope' this finds you well.* The penmanship looked like a mess, a scrawl wobbling with hesitation and the tremolo of his disorder. He closed the card and looked again at the cover. It was stupid. He tore the card in half and dropped it on the floor.

The dispatcher called out his unit number. She said, "County located your suspect vehicle, RO Aidon Clype. PNB interior."

Every fuse in Tom's body fired. Damn it to hell. PNB. Pulseless non-breather. Clype was dead, if it was Clype. Now Tom felt singed inside. The rising hum of anxiety in his ears cut into the transmission. "Tango," he said. "Come again."

"Nineteen frontage road north of Niwot, between Eighty-third and Airport."

Tom's foot punched the pedal of his vehicle, and it leaped forward. The location was fifteen minutes away. "Request standby for City of Boulder." He made a three-pointer to head to Diagonal. "Arrival in fifteen." He turned on lights and sirens, running berries and cherries like a blue flamer, but he needed a fast exit from this damned city.

Hell. Tom wanted to make an incision in himself so the sulfuric disappointment would leak out. Because there is no justice in a mere death. Simply slinking out. Everybody can die. He had wanted desperately to bring Clype in, to be the one to expose him to the fists of the system.

When he and Nate had gone up to the Fullarton residence for the death notification, one of the worst things was not being able to tell the mother, "Here she is, right here. I've got your beautiful little bird in here"—with a tap on his chest so light he wouldn't wake the nestling from her nap.

Then later, he'd planted himself in front of his screen and sifted through surveillance of every vehicle entering the rear parking area of the school, from the evening before to the end of that day, and he'd latched on to the pickup truck because he had a feeling about it. A few days later, they'd confirmed Clype as the suspect when the saliva specimen from her autopsy matched his DNA profile from an older case. Clype had been questioned, but no charges were brought. Nothing probative. They'd tried like hell to track him down. All the while, Tom's heart was getting eaten away by the little bird.

He exited the highway at Eighty-third, listened to the burble as his tires crossed the railroad tracks, and pulled onto the frontage road. Less than a mile on, he approached the scene. Two sheriff's cruisers sat kissing mirrors, the deps talking, gusts of breath rising, laughter. Tom drove past them and nosed in behind the truck registered to Clype—the target he had sought to bring to account.

Whatever man he'd been once, Tom was some other thing now—a thing not properly assembled anymore. The pieces were tethered to each other by wires, but afloat and incongruous. Quaking hands shoved into his coat pockets, he made pleasantries with the deputies, laughed even, and took ownership of the scene. But as he turned to inspect the vehicle, he felt he might piss or retch, or his legs might detach at the joints, and he would founder because he was some kind of take-apart dummy impersonating an officer.

On the rear gate of the truck, a bumper sticker read "Honk if you want to suck my dick." Tom went livid inside at the filth of it. That would have felt like reason enough to blow Clype away if he'd found him sooner.

He neared the driver's side and tugged a glove onto his shaking hand. He opened the door. Upon visual, anger bloomed in him, and he tried to repressurize his lungs. It was Clype. Long dead. Still frozen. A corpsicle. Tom decided he would say that word once he got back so everyone would laugh and think he really did have a sense of humor.

The body. Shirt unbuttoned. Blue-skin face. Mouth rimmed in the foam of an overdose. Too easy an escape. Tom had wanted more than anything to illuminate for Clype what a piece of crap he was, devastate him with enlightenment, and then exile him to a system that would take revenge upon him.

But Clype had skipped out free into the vale.

Tom's fingers crawled along his holster, allowed him the comfort of the cold grip of his Sig. He tasted a coppery impulse to fire all his rounds into the ice-blue chest. Next best thing. Desecrate and ventilate. For a second, his tremors stilled and he felt better.

But you may not, he thought. *You may not. Vengeance is mine, sayeth the system. Preserve this piece of crap for CSI like it's priceless.* He leaned in and inspected the face. Iceberg-blue, corneas dark, mouth gaping. Drool and vomitus and foam frozen around the purple lips and down the scruff on the chin. A lap full of vomit, a dark stain of urine in the crotch of the jeans. No blood. No violence done upon him. No righteousness carried out.

Beccs would catch this one. This was still Boulder County. She would divest the corpse of its cohesion. His mind flashed with the shine of stainless steel as he pictured not Clype, but himself on her table. If she snipped all the wires that held him together, it would be easy. Pieces and parts. He would happily watch her work as she opened him up. She'd peel back all the damage and look inside. If she saw his heart, she would see the grievous harm done to it, and maybe she would understand. Maybe she could. He visualized her surprise, and a moment when she might look so pleased when she discovered that ounce-weight bird, still fluttering deep inside there, and she'd know that he'd saved the little girl after all.

Look at yourself, Tom, he thought. *You're shaking like a damned jackhammer.* He glanced at the two sheriff's vehicles. *Are you going to come apart in front of a couple of county deps?*

Pain struck high behind his ribs like a tuning fork deep inside his chest wall. The sharp jab of something related to his tremors. *PDR, Tommy—pretty damn real.*

Sweating like a worked beast in the freezing air, he turned away from the truck and consciously instructed his legs to get him back to his own vehicle. *Left, right. Left, right.*

Hurry up. Equatorial fricking heat. The half-ton of dead-weight descended on his chest, and his first thought was that it might crush her. He had to retreat and find some air to breathe. Deep breaths. Had to sit down. Pain of the tuning fork traveling through his neck and down his back. *Left, right, left, right. Time to puke, I think. Hurry now. Sit.* He crumpled into his cruiser and slammed the door.

Chapter Thirty-Seven

～

6:00 PM
November 1, 2022 | Three Dog Knight Mine

Erin and Korrie found themselves facing the narrowing of a tunnel.

Shivering hard, Korrie leaned against Erin's sleeve and asked, "How did you find me, Mommy?"

This was the second time Korrie had asked. Erin looked at the scared pink face of her child in the phantom light of her phone and then at the same face in the background image on the dim, splintered display. Erin had no idea how much to tell Korrie, how much she could understand when Erin didn't understand it herself, and she knew she had to keep her calm.

"Remember?" Erin said, "I told you how I followed his tracks." Korrie blinked with confusion. Erin added, "From school."

"He is a horrible man!" Korrie's voice broke when she said it.

"I know," Erin said, rubbing Korrie's shoulder, "but he can't follow us here." And she believed that was true.

Korrie looked unconvinced. "Where are we?"

"Remember I said this used to be a mine once upon a time?" With a few more steps, Erin saw in the light of her phone that the tunnel had dead-ended.

Between red beats of the low-battery alert, the display read 6:00 PM and still November 1, 2022. Had they truly skipped forward now? By months and months? She turned back to face in the direction they'd come from. "We just have to find our way out."

Korrie nudged her arm. "Mommy, I feel weird."

Erin dropped to her knees. "In what way, baby?"

"Floaty and sideways-y." Korrie tried to wipe her cheek against the shoulder of the hoodie. "Dizzy."

It was closing in on them, the repetition of events. Erin breathed in the sharp, icy air and raised her aching hand and put a knuckle under Korrie's chin. "That's what we're going to fix. We're going to get out of here and get in the car and drive fast, fast, fast to the doctor."

"Okay," Korrie nodded.

They hurried through the dust into the widening of the frozen tunnel.

Erin tried to sequence things in her mind. Her car was parked in summer, where they would have to find it as soon as this interval ended. Once they got to the hospital, the medical staff would take care of Korrie, and Erin would call the police, call Zac, and then they could take care of her own injuries. Probably stitches in her back, she judged, from the resounding sting of it. Broken fingers. Splintered breastbone. Whatever else. Somehow, she would explain all of this. The question right now was, if time had skipped all this way forward, did that buy Korrie more time or give her less? How could Erin figure it out? All she could do was pay attention to Korrie's condition. Right now, she was still able to walk. So sometime early in the exposure to the oxycodone?

The tunnel made an L-turn, and in another fifty feet it ended in the squared-off housing of sets of pulleys that hung by shredded rope. Wrong way.

"What if we can't get out," Korrie said. Her eyes wide and the corners sunk down in fear.

Erin cleared her own doubt out of her voice and said, "We can do it, Squid. We can find a way out."

They headed back past the L-turn, and Erin tried to think of ways to reassure Korrie. "When we get home," she said, "you can have a nice hot dinner and then a warm bath." Erin was struck by how odd it sounded to talk about such ordinary things. "You can snuggle up under the covers, and we'll read for a little while."

"But Mommy?" she said, teeth chattering. She seemed to doubt Erin's assessment.

Erin felt a current against her cheek. "Wait, stop," she said, and she put up a hand in front of Korrie's chest.

"What?" Korrie said.

"Do you feel that?" Erin turned her head.

"What?" Korrie looked up at her.

"That must be the wind," she said and faced it. "That's the way out, Squid."

Goosebumps prickled along her bare arms. Relief rolled through her, and she felt almost certain inside. The light of the phone blundered along the walls as they charged toward the current. From a narrow side passage, moving air brushed Erin's arms.

"Here we go," she said.

At the end of the passage, a decrepit black lattice, cross-hatches of charcoal, hung aslant. Erin rushed to it and kicked it down. Korrie approached from behind her and said, "You did it, Mommy."

They climbed over the splintered sections, out of the tunnel, and stepped into a frozen, decimated burnout. The cold of twilight seemed to suck the life out of Erin's bones. Before them in the feeble light lay a blasted landscape, the ground covered not with snow, but with the dry char that follows a devastating forest fire; no snow-burdened trees, but only black spires bristling over the surrounding hillsides—burnt trunks of bare aspen and pine, all spikes of carbon. The forest around the mine was utterly destroyed.

The idea occurred to Erin that maybe she had caused this, but she shut her mind against it.

She drew out her phone, but it didn't wake. She pressed the button harder. No illumination at all. Her phone was dead.

"Where do we go now?" Korrie said.

"It's okay." Erin patted her back. "We just have to wait for it to change."

"What?" Korrie looked up at her. "What do you mean?"

Erin couldn't answer. *It should be summer by now, shouldn't it?* Tension pulled tight across Erin's chest. She thought back. They'd been within an interval of the past when she faced Clype, and then they'd suddenly ended up here, where time had skipped forward into some future, and there had been no return to summer.

She focused on Korrie's bewildered face. With a quick breath, she said, "We've got to keep moving, Squid. We have to get you to the car." There was no time to sort it out. She would file the facts for later and let Zac decipher what it all meant. She gauged the slope of the charred peaks around them. The burn area seemed to stretch in every direction. She estimated that she and Korrie had come out of the mine shaft north and west of the mill. They had to scale the incline directly ahead and hopefully head downhill from there to get back to the old road.

Korrie's bare feet shone the color of little white mushrooms against the cold, sooty earth. She shivered and pulled her shoulders up to her ears.

"Here you go," Erin said, kneeling down. "Here are your socks." She pulled them from her pocket.

Korrie raised a foot and said, "You got my socks back."

As Erin slipped the second sock onto Korrie's other foot, she realized how impossible it would be to explain any of this to her. When Korrie put her foot down, she swayed and nearly lost her balance. "I'm going to carry you, Korrie." Erin knelt back-first at Korrie's feet. "All aboard, Squid."

But Korrie cried, "Oh, Mommy, there's lots of blood. You're bleeding."

"Korrie, I'm okay. We have to hurry. Climb up, quick." She folded as low and flat as she could so Korrie could squirm aboard piggyback, using just her legs. Erin winced at the sharp sting of the wound as Korrie pressed close and wrapped her bare legs around Erin's waist.

She slid her arms underneath Korrie, pulling the hoodie down so it would at least cover her underwear, and locked the child in place with her left hand clamped around her right wrist. Her hands crackled like splintered matchwood, bones in fragments. Pain lit bright and sharp, and a cry slipped out.

"I'm sorry," Korrie sobbed.

Erin made her voice steady and calm. "We're okay, Squid. Let's go." With a searing shrug, she hiked Korrie higher and stepped forward into the parched char.

Chapter Thirty-Eight

≈

Zac circled his finger on the "Enter" key, but he didn't press it. If he simply ran the sim again, he would get only the same result.

Erin.

His heart knocked around, lost in his chest, and meanwhile his mind hunted, but his thinking refused to come together. It was as if an oar was intermittently dipped into the water, disturbing the surface, calling his focus away from the glass in front of him.

Erin.

It was as if he were listening for her, and though he couldn't see her in the water, each dip of the oar sent ripples toward Erin, swimming her way back to him.

He drove a pen frantically across a page of his notebook, the black ink streaking across the path of mathematical journeys forged by other men. He prayed for them to prove today wrong. Because if what he was seeing was true, it would mean that the life remembered is only an abridged re-creation of life lived, a Frankensteined butterfly stitched together from survivor fragments. It would mean that there were moments in his life with Erin that had been stolen. Moments stolen from everyone.

Zac crossed out the equation he'd written, but when he tried again, it repeated itself. Every attempt ended in extinction of everything that inhabited the gap.

Walter stood and shook out his hands. "Let's see where we are in another hour." Everyone looked at him in disbelief. Waiting an hour would not solve the impossible position they found themselves in. If anything, it would only become more of what it was. Walter surveyed their faces. "Let's humor each other. Let's let it stew for a while."

Mark tapped on his desktop to get Zac's attention and nodded toward the door of the Clean Room. Out in the fluorescence beyond the glass, on top of the property lockers, Zac's phone was a rectangle of light. He sprinted, pulled up short when the doors didn't open fast enough, ran to the lockers, grabbed the phone. Erin? Dan? It was Dan.

Zac answered. "Hey," he said.

"So, um . . ." Dan said. He took a deep breath. "I'm here."

"And?" *Why so slow, little brother? What is it?*

"And . . . I don't know," he drawled.

"So," Zac said. "Is she there?"

"No, but . . ."

"But what, Dan—Christ, what is it?"

"She's not here. Her car's not here."

He was like a mule that wouldn't go through a gate. "Okay . . ."

"And things are kind of interrupted-looking, I guess. Like she left in a hurry. There's stuff spread out. There are eggs and stuff left out on the counter."

"Okay, so it's kind of—"

"So there's this note. Looks pretty weird. Like . . . morbid, Zac."

"A note from Erin? What does it say?" He wanted to snap his fingers to hurry Dan along.

"I don't know. Different times written down and Korrie's name and maybe a casket."

Zac felt a sharp inhale as if a cold wave had splashed up his bare chest.

"It says 'To Korrie first.'" Dan made a humph sound. "Strange. Haphazard. I'm sending a picture."

"Okay, thanks," Zac made a fist of his other hand and released it, but the tension remained.

"Sure," Dan said. "I'll lock up. Call me whenever."

"Could you please keep trying to reach her?" Zac said. "Leave me a message when you talk to her?"

"You bet," Dan said.

Zac held his phone face up in his palm until Dan's photo of the note arrived. It showed a page in Erin's strung-out hand. The date, a smattering of times, and an arrow pointing down to what Dan had described as Korrie's casket. Lines making a box around her name. *Ah, damn,* Zac thought, *poor Erin.* Submerged in that current, the rip current of her mind. No escape for her. Alone there in all that. He didn't want to drown with her, but he wanted to be there where he could hold on to her, his once beloved. Still beloved.

On his phone, he touched the image of her face, the younger version of Erin, her face undiluted joy. The number rang a few times until the phone beeped with a notification that the call had failed.

He looked through the glass into the Clean Room, at Mark hunched at his keyboard in frustration. Working toward the improbable, maybe counting on Zac to rejoin him and help him bring sense to it.

What words had Zac and Erin said to each other that they couldn't now recall because the memory was swept away when a fragment of time was ripped to pieces by a passing gravitational wave? How many? Maybe that was the question he should be asking. Not "how is this possible?," but "how much is possible?" How much was lost as the waves rolled over a lifetime and stole wisps from it? A second? A minute? More? And could this question explain anything about Erin? About her empty message? He repositioned his phone on its perch. There was nothing to do but wait.

With a new sense of what had to be done, he put on another pair of coveralls and reentered the Clean Room. Until Dan found Erin and one of them called him, all he could do was work. In the time remaining, he had to figure out what was left of a life once physics was done with it.

Chapter Thirty-Nine

❦

November 1, 2022 | Three Dog Knight Mining Mill

Erin trudged with Korrie on her back through the bitter twilight in the direction of the moon above the horizon. It had been too long since the last shift to summer. Time was just one long stretch of *this* time, this windswept wreckage of a fire-ravaged November. It took longer than Erin expected to reach the mill. When she slowed, Korrie shifted against her. The clutter of blackened tree trunks thinned, and the blown-apart building appeared. The mangled graphite framework loomed aslant.

"Is that the place I was, Mommy?" Korrie murmured. Her speech was slurred. "What happened to it?"

"It's hard to explain." Erin's breath hung suspended in the air. "Daddy will tell us when we get home."

"Daddy is home?"

"Maybe," Erin said, rushing past the twisted husk of the structure. She'd forgotten that for Korrie, Zac had never moved out. In her chronology, he was on his way back from his trip to Hingoli. But that was in a different winter, one from the past, one that was no longer repeating. "We'll call him when we get to the hospital."

But how could she call him if he was living in their true time, in summer, in a time that stood months behind this winter of the future?

"Hos-pital," Korrie said. Was her speech slowed by the cold or by the oxycodone? Erin clattered down the slope, through the burnt-out aspen grove, toward the road. Fighting to keep her balance as Korrie drooped first to one side and then the other, Erin half-cantered, half-skidded through the scree to the pavement.

She squinted into the distance, along the slender carpet of ash, to where she'd parked. She hurried on, but she could tell before she got much closer that the car was destroyed. She approached it, saw how it squatted flat on the roadbed. The body of the car was an empty, blackened shell—windows no more than heaps of shattered pieces on the pavement, tires burned away.

She stopped. Everything inside her drained away.

"What, Mommy?" Korrie asked.

"The car," Erin said without thinking.

"The car?" Korrie said. Erin felt her straining to raise herself higher, to see better. "Our car?"

Erin sank to her knees and sat back on her heels. She unclamped her hands, unfolded her arms, and let Korrie down onto the asphalt. "Our car."

Korrie took two steps forward through the wind-blown ash. She turned and faced Erin, her eyes flooding. "How will we get to the hospital?"

Erin couldn't speak.

"Am I going to die?" Korrie cried.

Erin knelt, paralyzed. *Yes,* was the answer that sprang into her mind. Hope slipped from her like a pearl down the drain. Nothing remained.

"Mommy, am I going to die?" Korrie threw herself against Erin's chest.

Erin couldn't breathe. Her chest ached where Clype had stomped on it. Her eyes welled, and tears blurred her vision. Space, syrupy around her, slowed her movements. She carefully wrapped her arms around Korrie. A child as delicate as the wispy-winged tissue creatures she made in art class. The purest good nature of anything Erin had ever known.

The temperature was plunging, the way it does on clear winter evenings once the light fails. A steel sky—Venus and Jupiter and a half-moon. The dry, bone-chilling current of icy air like an aggression against them. They would not last much longer, exposed like this.

Some voice inside her said she should take Korrie back to the shelter of the mine and get her out of the wind and build a fire for her so at least she would be warm. It would be the kindest thing. Maybe the only thing. At least she would be able to lie down somewhere as the drug coursed through her, closed her eyes, stopped her heart. Darkening her world into nothingness. Erin could hold her on her lap and give her comfort. Let her go, let her rest somewhere where she would feel safe and warm.

"Mommy?" Korrie cried.

If Erin still saw herself as that ghost who lived in those white woods, she would have felt her history pulling inward, its gravity so intense that no memory could escape it, so dense no reflection could penetrate it, her spirit shrinking into a tiny pinpoint of darkness. But that was not who Korrie needed. She needed grit and willpower.

Erin raised her head, pulled against the aches of her battered body, rose onto her knees, and said, "Of course not, Squid." She straightened Korrie in front of her with the backs of her wrists. "We're still going to get you to the hospital." She angled herself with her back toward Korrie and gestured with the shrug of her shoulder. "I carried you here; I can carry you there." She heard her own voice as if it were steady and self-certain and almost Seussian in its lilt. "Hurry, Korrie. We have to hurry."

Korrie wept hard, said, "Okay," as she leaned against Erin's spine, skin tugging downward, a blade of pain as the wound refreshed itself. Erin repositioned her, and, despite her ruined hands, she drew the loose sleeves of the hoodie under her own arms and tied the cloth like a sling across her bruised chest. She locked her hand around her wrist beneath Korrie's seat again and, focusing all the determination she had into her spent legs, she raised herself to her feet.

Chapter Forty

~

November 1, 2022 | Spring Canyon

The burn scar seemed horrendous, its extent visible even as nightfall settled into the hills. From the scenic overlook, Erin had taken stock of the damage and estimated that some time ago a forest fire had ripped its way at least as far as Chautauqua Park on the southwest side of town, maybe farther. What was once forest was now black stubble of long-dead trees on the slopes. The grid of the city's lights blinked, but the boundary was much farther off than it should have been, as distant as the strings of headlights on the highway. Red beacons flashed at the tips of construction cranes.

Erin struggled now against the raw cold stiffening in her legs as she marched in the rising glow of the moon, following the trail through the wasteland of burned and fallen trees. She and Zac had hiked along this green stretch of trail so many times, first with Korrie in her baby sling and then in her carrier backpack and then on foot, past Bluebell, past the quarry, and back toward the NIST service road, the straightest way from the trailhead to the NIST campus where they usually parked, maybe four miles. How fast could she make the hike now?

Korrie's cheek pressed against the back of her shoulder. Erin shrugged lightly against her. "You have to stay awake, okay?"

"I can't," Korrie muttered.

"Yes, you can." Erin shifted Korrie's weight, noting that her own wound stung less now and that her hand hurt less because it was going numb. "You have to."

"No, that's okay." Korrie sounded dreamy and dull.

"You have to keep talking to me, Korrie. We'll do a story."

"I don't want to." Korrie's voice began to fade. "I feel bad."

"The trick is to keep going, no matter how you feel," Erin said, despite the rattle of her own rising alarm bell. "That's how it has to be." She gave her a gentle squeeze. "You start."

"Once there was . . . an elf," Korrie said.

"Who lived in the woods," Erin added.

She walked fast, cutting corners at curves in the trail, shaving seconds where she could. What kind of universe was this, that she would be given this second chance, if everything still fell apart and she couldn't save her child? Were the mistakes she made this time just of a greater scale? Were she and Korrie going to die of hypothermia out here in some strange future winter? Wasn't it ever going to turn back to summer again?

The air burned its arctic irons into her skin. Her breath frosted on her lips. She shivered so hard that it nearly made her lose her balance. Her legs grew heavier and clumsier. Korrie kept drifting, her five-word sentences trailing into three or two or nothing but murmurs.

Erin prompted her again. "Come on, Korrie, stay with me. What did the elf find after that?"

"A nice, soft, sleepy nest . . ."

"But," Erin added, "she was wide awake."

Eventually, Korrie stopped talking and Erin stopped shivering. She walked steadily for a stretch, and then she staggered and had to stand still long enough to reset herself. The trail quivered like a mirage before her, almost with the same strange rhythm as the manic fluttering of her heart. Part of her knew she was slipping into hypothermic confusion, but still, she thought, *I'm having a backwards pregnancy. I'm carrying the baby opposite of before. Zac will help me breathe,* she thought, *but if I have to give birth through the spinal canal, where will they put the epidural?* She flapped her free hand to see if it might fly away and go get help, but it was numb and quiet, and she couldn't tell if it moved or not. Sharp peaks of iridescence spiked in her peripheral vision. They disappeared when she turned her head, but they returned when she closed her eyes. What point was there in sticking to the trail? There were no trees left, only shadows, and who couldn't walk through a shadow? She stepped off the trail and followed the shadows as they marched forward down the slopes. But then they leaned in behind her, too close to Korrie, and she decided they were not trustworthy. *I don't understand my thinking.* Her heart fluttered more quietly, and she felt as if the night were bearing down on her and she was sinking into some smaller space in the world. *Pull yourself together,* she thought, *and get back on the trail.*

Just keep going, she repeated to herself, over and over until it was like a meditation. Korrie dangled limply. *Slipping from the broomsticks of my handles. Not handles. Not hands. Arms,* she told herself. The trail wove away in front of her, like a creek running in a storm. *Straighten yourself out and hold on. Don't let go.*

Chapter Forty-One

⌒

7:15 PM
Sunday, June 20, 2021 | National Institute of Standards and Technology

The Clean Room was somber and uncomfortably warm. Walter had emailed Schacht that they'd have an explanation soon, and he sat next to Zac, with his arms crossed, the heel of one foot bouncing with his impatience. They'd waited in silence for a long time for Mark and Jin to finalize this critical reconfiguration of the sim: the prediction of what would happen to the white hole at the ultimate moment when the two blast fronts tore into each other over its location. Zac suspected that he knew the outcome, but he kept his fears to himself and waited for the corroboration of the sim.

"Lights out, ladies," Jin said. He tapped a key three times on his keyboard and stood. Zac stood too.

Mark said, "Well, let's just see what we've got." His voice sounded tired. Then he looked at Jin and said, "Oh, you mean the actual lights." He rose. His feet scuffed against the tiles as he crossed to turn off all but one work light. He returned and situated himself near Zac's dock. The three of them stood together, waiting for Walter to join them, but he stayed in his seat.

On the large screen, the sim brightened. The creamy wavelets of the white hole sea lapped toward them. Strewn over the surface, a vast population of refractive beads bobbed and glittered, like a great flock of lights at peace. Walter sighed.

"Here's where we are," Mark said, and he laced his fingers at the back of his neck. "So we've got the evidence that gravitational waves create micro-rips in time and that the contents of the gap do not survive. But it might be . . . well, let's just see . . ." He let the silence resume.

Zac watched as the wavelets grew larger and moved faster toward the perspective of the viewer, as if a storm were gathering. The beads seemed to dim and scatter toward the upper quadrant of the image.

"Give me one good reason to put that in," Walter said, "like there's something coming after them."

"We didn't put it in," Jin said. "It's the sim trying to find an analogy for the interactions."

"Watch this," Mark said. "As the white hole drives everything away from its core, tidal forces at the horizon reflect in both directions simultaneously. A mirror of past to present and present to future." Mark looked intently at Zac and then at Jin. "Unfathomable, right?"

As the storm became more violent, huge white swells dropping the stranded beads into deep troughs, Zac stepped closer to the screen. The point of view of the sim drew backward to the outside of the white hole's exit horizon. The beads of light mirrored at the border were torn apart, and they exploded one after another in fatal blasts of radiation.

The sim zoomed out from the white hole and revealed the approach in the distance of two enormous opposing waves. The blast fronts. Zac's hands balled into fists, and he shoved them into the pockets of his coveralls as the waves climbed the screen, closing in over the white hole, huge raging cliff faces rushing at each other.

At the moment of collision, the screen flashed explosive white and then went black.

Nothingness.

Zac blinked at the darkness.

Walter flipped on the monitor next to him, and when the guys turned, it threw a blue glow over their faces. "And?" he said.

Wrestling against the ponderous heft of it, Zac said, "That's it."

With a tinge of hostility, Walter said, "That's what?"

Zac heaved out all the breath in his chest. "That's the sim trying to show us what will happen."

"Which is what?" Walter said, as if to accuse Zac of some kind of trick.

Zac stood up to him as well as he could, but he felt as if he'd taken a blow. "The entire thing is obliterated. The white hole will be gone."

Walter hunched forward with his elbows on his knees. When he looked up, he said, "Let's be realistic. This could simply be a metaphor for something we've screwed up."

"I don't think so," Zac said, even though he wished that were the case. Exhaustion weighed on him, and he sat again next to Walter.

Walter patted his arm. "Let's do this: Let's step back and find a different way to look at it. Shift our perspective. Can we do that, please?"

"Sure," Zac sighed, futility taking all the fight out of his tone.

"Guys?" Walter pressed Mark and Jin for their agreement.

"Why not?" Jin said, and he and Mark retreated to their posts.

Zac faced his monitor. His intellect sped down the track in one direction, but his emotions circled, separate. With each flash of the seconds indicator in the corner of his screen, with each glance through the glass of the doors toward the dark face of his phone, he was more and more aware that Dan hadn't been able to find Erin.

Two worries circled each other—one, that she'd done something insane, and another, that something had happened to her, that she was somehow missing.

He tried to clear a space in his mind and visualize that bizarre note Erin had written. What could all of that mean? Today's date, that scatter of times. Was that some sort of countdown? A countdown to what? Korrie in her box. "To Korrie first?" First, before what? God, she wasn't planning to do something to herself, was she? Maybe he should call Dr. Tanner. But what could he do?

Dan had thought the box was a casket.

In Green Mountain.

Zac stood so quickly his chair skittered away across the tile floor of the Clean Room. "Guys," he said, "I'll be right back."

Walter stood. "What now, Zac?" Chin tucked, body stout and adamant, he looked like a Tyvek-clad bull. "What is the problem now?"

Zac felt cold rising as if from somewhere below him. He couldn't take the time to grapple with Walter's opinions. "I think Erin's in trouble," he said, heading toward the door.

"So that's what we're doing?" Walter stopped him with the force of his tone. He made a gesture with his hands palms up and open wide. "We're dropping the most important work that's ever been done for some domestic melodrama?"

Zac met him head-on. "I need a few minutes."

"For what?" He cocked his head. "To indulge her fixation? I don't think you're doing her any favors."

"What does that mean?" Zac snapped.

Walter shrugged a shoulder. "I'm telling you, it probably doesn't do her any good for you to coddle her. In fact, it probably makes her worse. I mean, when I saw her outside this morning, she looked like a lunatic."

A frigid shock ran down Zac's body. "Outside?"

"Yes," Walter said, guiltily defensive. "Earlier. Saying all this stuff about your—your tragedy . . ."

Zac couldn't slow the anger that flew out of him. "Fuck, Walter! She was here? And you didn't tell me?" All the glass in the room seemed to shudder at the volume.

Jin and Mark sat watching, as if unable to look away from a wreck in slow motion. Walter's chin jutted, his lips parted as if he meant to smile. "She wanted to get into the building to talk to you. Just nuts. And in front of Schacht too."

"How could you not tell me!" Overwhelmed, Zac pulled his fingers through his hair. "I can't believe you said *nothing*!"

"Wow." Walter stepped back. "You are really overreacting."

"Fuck, Walter!" Zac said, "For *hours* you said nothing!" and he slid through the doors and tore off his coveralls.

When he grabbed his phone off the top of the property lockers, it was powered on but there had been no calls. No contact. As he sped toward the exit, he tapped his phone to call Erin's number. The call failed. He had to get out of the building and cross the street and go to Green Mountain. To Korrie's grave. Maybe Erin had gone there. Maybe that's what her note was about. Trying to be close to Korrie.

He shoved through the doors and out into the ivory light of the summer evening. The campus was deserted, quiet, pulsing with calls of cicadas, a slight smell of smoke in the air, a cloudless sky. He ran to the back gate, slipped around the security arm, and crossed the road into the green peace of the cemetery. Running down the main path, he passed row upon row of headstones, their long shadows touching in unbroken chains.

The path curved and then forked in front of a pine grove, and he took the gravel walkway toward the spot where Korrie lay in her grave. There was no sign of Erin. He scanned the entire layout of this section of the cemetery. Nothing moved. No sign of anyone. He listened, but there were no sounds except the rhythmic droning of the insects.

Ahead, at the end of the row, was Korrie's headstone. Blue granite, inscribed with the silhouette of a dove and her name and her dates, the inscription. His father had helped him choose the stone. The two men had nearly had a nervous breakdown, having to sit in the funeral director's office and look through the endless options. It all seemed like a mockery of the unreality they were trapped in. Teddy bears, angel wings, and syrupy, sentimental epitaphs.

The funeral director, after a long wait while they sat frustrated and incapable of deciding, asked them, "Which one do you think little Korrie would have liked?"

A hideous, bitter laughter had slipped from Zac's lips. His father looked horrified and stood as if he could shield Zac.

They'd eventually chosen the epitaph "Casting off one shore to find another yet undreamed." And now Zac wondered what that had meant to him then. What had he been thinking? Poor Korrie, saddled with his confusion for all time. But her dying had been so confusing. Still was, even now.

Dusk arrived slowly at this point of summer—the solstice. Zac gazed at the stretch of green leading to the Flatirons and the Rockies beyond, a weary, romantic texture created by the severe angle of the light. Old peaks worn down almost smooth. What histories had they witnessed that had been snatched out of existence by a passing wave? How, in the course of a day, this mere day, had the impossible become the truth?

He crossed his arms and let his gaze linger over the name on the stone. Erin had decided to take his name when they got married, said she loved the old Scottish sigil of his clan, the motto—*Lux in tenebris, light into darkness*—and they'd chosen the baby's name only seven weeks into the pregnancy. Korrie Andrea Fullarton. *Still a pretty name for you, down there in the dark.*

Lux in tenebris—that's what he should have put on the stone. Why hadn't he thought of that? Because he couldn't think. Still could hardly think.

And now he had to get back to the Clean Room. *Go deal with Walter,* he told himself. Nothing here could help him find Erin. He had to turn away from the reddening sun, away from the green hills, and get back to the vortex of his work—the betrayal by his friend, and the breaking news, when they released it, that would splinter everyone's idea of their lifetime.

Chapter Forty-Two

~

November 1, 2022 | Southwest Approach to Green Mountain Cemetery

In the last hint of light, Erin searched for the NIST service road. Where it should have been, a collapsed slide of frozen mud and torn branches sloped into the ravine. Erin's ice-bitten legs were cumbersome and unmanageable beneath her as she stumbled toward Green Mountain.

Beyond the ravine, the open field lay before her, moon-washed pale and smooth, and she had the odd sensation that the earth was reaching up to meet the soles of her boots, impact against the liners where she should have been able to feel her footfalls, but the ache had stopped as if her feet had disappeared. Korrie slumped against her back.

The cemetery rose ahead of her. She took deep frozen breaths to sharpen her dull mind. She would have to cut through the graveyard to get to the NIST campus, to get to the phone at the back security gate. Nothing remained of the landscape as she'd last seen it. The half-moon laid down a vague wash of dusty light on all the rows of stones. All the trees were gone, and in their place were small, desiccated stumps. The building where the cemetery's office had been was gone. A front-loader sat at the end of one of the rows where the wide path led past Korrie's plot, her headstone. Erin's mind struggled with the idea. She was stricken by the thought that fire might have damaged Korrie's headstone, and yet here was Korrie, still alive, with her. She hurried up the path until she reached Korrie's plot, her blue granite stone, the dove, the words. How was this even possible?

She rounded the curve in the path and searched the terrain ahead. Across the road from the cemetery, there was a skeletal construction of a new building framed up next to the NIST lab.

In the distance, it looked as if there was a dim little shard of light. She hurried to where she could see it better. Yes. A construction trailer. There was a light.

"Look, Korrie," she said, "the light's on."

Korrie murmured back to her, but Erin couldn't make out the words.

"What, baby?" she said.

Korrie's voice, only a hoarse whisper, "My feet on fire?"

Erin looked down at the small pink socks against her thighs. "I'm so sorry, sweetie," she said. The socks had been all she had to warm Korrie's feet. When she'd pulled them out of her pocket—

Oh, no, Erin thought. The ring. What had happened to her ring when she'd pulled out the socks? She balanced Korrie with her good hand and reached her battered hand into her pocket. The ring was still there. It was not lost. *Okay.* She thumbed the ring onto her swollen little finger. Zac's time crystal. Thinking his name brought up his beautiful face. Remorse swirled through her. All those months since she'd driven him away, he'd been alone. She was the only person who could feel what he'd been going through, but she'd sent him off to deal with it by himself.

She would return Korrie to him now and all would be forgiven. She nudged Korrie with her shoulder. "Squid?" There was no response. "Korrie," Erin said, "wake up." She jostled her, tried to look back at her face. "Wake up."

The warm, golden light of blinding summer suddenly radiated all around them. Green grass and trees glowed with vibrancy, and the scent of pine saturated the air.

"Oh thank God!" Erin cried.

She rushed forward through the tangerine of dusk, toward the far edge of the cemetery grounds.

"Korrie," she said, "it's okay now."

The interval had finally changed. They glided forward in the sublime kindness of summer.

"Squid." She shrugged against Korrie's cheek with her shoulder, but there was no answer. "Korrie," she said louder, "you have to wake up."

Her hands tingled with life, and the feeling in her feet was returning like a vise grip as they thawed, but she couldn't get a sound from Korrie. She stopped, untied the arms of the hoodie, and lowered herself to her knees. Clumsy still as her hands warmed, she slid Korrie off her back. Pouring from Erin's grasp, her body was like liquid. Her face was the color of frost, there in the balmy, creamy light. Her lips were blue.

"No, no, no!" Erin cried. She put her ear to Korrie's chest. She heard nothing but her own pulse rushing in her ears. "Korrie," she cried. She put her maimed hand on Korrie's cheek. "Breathe." She watched for a moment to see if her chest moved. Nothing. She tilted Korrie's head back, pressed her lips around those open blue lips, and forced in a whoosh of air. She watched and saw Korrie's chest fall, but it didn't rise again. "Come on," she begged, "please." She leaned over again and blew in another breath.

Chapter Forty-Three

༄

Zac felt the heat of the low western sun soaking through the back of his shirt as he approached the curve where the stand of pines lined the cemetery pathway. He decided that if he didn't hear from Dan in the next few minutes, he would call Erin's doctor. Maybe she'd told him things Zac didn't know about. He was startled out of the cyclone of his thoughts when he saw a figure hunched in the middle of the path. A woman with hair like Erin's knelt there, leaning over a small body. With horror, he recognized that it actually was Erin. And that the body was Korrie's.

He pulled up short, paralyzed. "Erin?" he called.

Her head jerked upward. Confusion and recognition crossed her face. She looked crazed. "Zac!" she cried. "Call nine-one-one!"

He stepped toward her, faltering, feeling stunned, as if someone had shot him. "What have you done?" he said. He looked at the small body. His mind went scattershot, trying to understand what he was seeing. He saw his daughter, but he'd just stood moments ago at the untouched grave.

"Right now!" Erin screamed. "Call nine-one-one!"

He couldn't speak. He could only shamble, mystified, toward them. Erin leaned over and blew a breath into the body.

"My god, Erin, what are you doing?" His face goose-fleshed with sweat.

"Just do it," she yelled. "Call an ambulance! She's not breathing!" She put a hand on the child's chest, a hand mutilated, bloodied, crooked, and purple. She leaned in again and blew another breath. She sat back and looked down at the face. He looked too. His Korrie. Her jaw hung slack. Her lips were blue.

"Help me, Zac," Erin cried.

He crossed the last yard toward them through the thickening length of time it took to get close, and then he knelt opposite Erin. She looked insane, her eyes round and her brows tight. He looked at the body and reached his hand toward the face of his girl. He touched it. It was soft with the give of living flesh. Warm. The impossibility of it flashed through his mind.

Giving in, he pulled his phone from his pocket and pressed "Emergency." He watched his wife breathing rescue breaths into the motionless form of his daughter.

A male voice on his phone asked about the nature of his emergency.

"I need an ambulance." He sounded calm to himself, detached from the cataclysm his body was going through. The dispatcher asked about the location, and Zac answered, even though he disbelieved his own words. "Green Mountain Cemetery," he said, "where it borders Compton Road is the nearest street." It sounded as if someone else were speaking for him, his voice disembodied.

The dispatcher confirmed that he had their location and that paramedics were on the way and said Zac should remain on the line with him. "What's happening?" he said.

"My daughter's not breathing, and my wife's doing mouth-to-mouth." *Let the words go,* he thought. *Let them tell.* Because how could he answer otherwise?

Erin gave another breath and then straightened up. "Are they coming?"

"Yes," he told her. He grasped for some shred of comprehension. The dispatcher asked how old his daughter was. He looked at Korrie, her skin still that smooth perfection of baby skin, freckles. "Six," he answered. But then he didn't know if that was right. What did it matter? When the dispatcher asked him what had happened, he couldn't answer. "I don't know," he said. That was all he was sure of.

The dispatcher coached Zac to let Erin continue giving rescue breaths and to take over if she got tired. "But paramedics should be on scene in a minute or so," he said. He told Zac how to check for a pulse at Korrie's neck, but Zac's body thumped with its own thrashing hysteria, and he couldn't tell if there was a beat. "I can't find it," he said.

"That's all right," the dispatcher said. "Don't do chest compressions then. Tell your wife to keep giving rescue breaths."

"Keep going," Zac told Erin, and she nodded.

The dispatcher asked Zac how long it had been since Korrie had stopped breathing, and all the crossings in his mind collided. Five hundred days? What kind of time was he in? What was real now? This? The official questions reared one at a time: What was her full name? What had occurred? Were there injuries? All Zac could say was that he didn't know.

When the sound of sirens whined in the distance, Zac said to the dispatcher, "We're on the grounds of the cemetery. We have to get her out toward the road."

"No, no, don't do that," he answered. "Don't move her. Let the paramedics come to you."

Zac found himself beginning to cry. Tears stung at the edges of his dry eyes. His throat seized shut. Relief softened inside his chest and he surrendered. Help was coming. Somehow, help was coming for Korrie.

He sprang to his feet as Erin bent over to give another breath. Down the back of her T-shirt, he saw blood in a huge red splotch. "Your back," he said. "My god, there's blood."

She shook her head. "I'm fine."

He turned toward the rising whine of the siren. "We're not supposed to move her. I'm going to show them where we are."

She leaned over Korrie again, and he took off running toward Compton, his thoughts like rocks in a tumbler. He reached the middle of the road, stopped, and looked toward the intersection. A red and white ambulance appeared from Rayleigh and raced toward him. He waved his arms until the woman and man inside signaled him to get out of the way. He jumped back onto the grass as they braked to a halt. The techs leaped from doors on each side of the ambulance. They swung open the back doors of the vehicle and yanked out a folded gurney.

"She's over here," Zac said, and he turned, sprinted, and led the paramedics to the spot where Erin still knelt over Korrie.

Before they even reached her, Erin started explaining, "I've been trying, but she's not breathing. It's been a long time."

She stood aside as the paramedics gloved up and leaned over Korrie. The one nearest her said, "Do we need a brace? For her neck, her back?"

"No," Erin said. "It's oxycodone. It's an overdose."

As the paramedics knelt beside Korrie, one of them tried to pull her arms out from under her. He rolled her on her side and saw the plastic cuffs and said, "Holy Jesus Christ." He looked up at Erin.

"She was abducted." She shivered and visibly cringed. "I couldn't get those off."

Zac's chest flooded with a father's instincts, and he wanted to let the violence inside him burst out.

The paramedics lifted Korrie's limp body onto the gurney and rushed off with her, speaking to each other in one-word sentences, letting Erin and Zac run behind.

Zac flushed as if a roller of pins and needles were running over him, shaking as if he would rip at the seams, his nerves blasting, the impact of an idea: the ascension of a wave—then crashing into the surface of time.

When they reached the ambulance, the paramedics loaded Korrie. The man leaped in back with her. Erin and Zac climbed into the tight confines around the gurney and squeezed themselves onto the tiny bench seat along the side. The other tech closed them inside and then appeared a second later in front of them, in the driver's seat.

As the ambulance lurched forward, the tech pulled a mask over Korrie's nose and mouth. He compressed the bag attached to it and then pressed two fingertips to her carotid.

"Is there a heartbeat?" Erin asked. She touched Zac's hand as the vehicle tipped around the corner and jostled them together on the seat.

The man looked at his watch. "There . . ." He paused. "There it is. Weak and thready. But yes, ma'am."

Erin's head fell forward and rested in her hands.

"You know for sure it's oxycodone?" he said.

She pulled herself up straight and wiped that ugly hand across her wet cheek. "Yes."

From a drawer above her, he pulled a small square device with a short nozzle. He pulled back the mask and pushed the tip of the device into Korrie's nostril.

"What's that?" Zac asked.

"Naloxone." The tech pressed the plunger. He repositioned the mask and compressed the bag. "To counteract the oxy." He unzipped the hoodie and rubbed Korrie's chest vigorously and called her name. "Wake up now," he yelled against the backdrop of the siren. One hand still over her heart, he reached with the other into a compartment under the seat and pulled out a large pair of shears. He rolled Korrie's shoulders enough that he could snip the heavy black plastic and free Korrie's wrists. He pulled the bands away, fetched a paper bag from one of the drawers, and dropped them in it, folding the top over. He tenderly straightened Korrie's arms at her sides before he pushed up her sleeve and inserted an IV line inside the bend of her elbow. He went back to rubbing her chest and saying her name. He sandwiched her hand between his and rubbed hard.

"Tell her to wake up," he instructed Erin, and he squeezed the bag on the mask again.

"Korrie," Erin said, "open your eyes." There was no response. She took Korrie's hand in hers. "Wake up, baby."

Zac noticed the tech's instant assessment of that bedraggled ruin of a hand, blood dried, shiny with swelling, bruised dark, fingers splaying at odd angles. Zac needed to unravel where she'd been and what the hell had happened.

The tech tipped his chin toward her hand and said to Erin, "We'll get to that."

She showed the tech a hint of a smile. Zac wanted to tell him about the wound on her back, but before he could gather the words, the tech moved aside Korrie's mask and gave her another plunger of the antidote. He pressed the chest piece of his stethoscope to her skin. "Better," he said.

Senseless with bewilderment and gratitude, Zac leaned forward and let the surf roll as he cupped his hands around those of his wife and his child.

Chapter Forty-Four

❧

8:25 PM
June 20, 2021 | Foothills Hospital Emergency Room

An orderly had wheeled Erin away to Radiology, and so Zac stayed with Korrie as she lay unconscious in the ER cubicle. After a few minutes, a woman in regular street clothes invaded the cubicle and introduced herself, though Zac couldn't have repeated what she said, intoxicated as he was with the return of his child back into his life. He was thinking about how long it would be before they brought Erin back to him so he could find out how she'd done it. The woman asked him for Korrie's information so she could fill in the form on her tablet. Date of birth, health history, immunizations, insurance. Korrie hadn't been on his insurance for sixteen months. He told the woman he couldn't answer her questions now and promised he would deal with it later, after they brought his wife back.

Alone again in their cubicle, he kissed Korrie's forehead and whispered her name. He sat beside her and looked at her face. Perfectly alive. Unconscious but breathing on her own. She'd had another dose of naloxone and would need another because the oxycodone was still circulating in her bloodstream. But her heart was beating, strong chirps sounding from the machine beside her. The monitor's green tracings leaped up into a neat row of peaks, steady and even. Zac took her hand in his. He pressed her pink fingers, like petals, against his lips. Remnants of glitter nail polish rimmed her cuticles, and he remembered thinking Erin could teach her how to take that off with a Q-tip—a thought retrieved from the night before he left for Hingoli, meaning that somehow Korrie had skipped all the months between then and now.

How could it be possible that any living person could break through a closed timelike curve, if that's what it was?

And where was Erin? It was past 8:30, and it seemed like they'd had her for X-rays for ages. How could he wait any longer to find out what had happened?

Just then, as if in answer to the wish, the orderly wheeled her into the cubicle, a hospital gown over her sweatpants and her hand bandaged into a round, white mitten. The orderly helped her stand and then took the wheelchair and left.

Zac stood, and his chest filled with lightness at the sight of her.

She held up her bandaged hand. "Three broken digits." She smiled.

His old Erin. He laid Korrie's hand on the sheet. With a step, he carefully gathered Erin into his arms.

"Ow," she laughed.

He stepped back. "What?"

She pulled the neckline of her hospital gown down between her breasts to reveal a deep purple bruise.

"What is that?" Zac said. "What happened to you?"

"It's a boot mark." She took his hand with her unbandaged one, and with a glimpse, he noted that oddly enough, her engagement ring was now on her swollen little finger. She turned toward Korrie. "She's doing okay?" she asked.

"Yeah," he said. "Good." In the back opening of the hospital gown, he could see layers of white bandaging. "What happened?" He returned to his question. "A boot mark?"

Everything blacked out. It was as if they'd stepped into a blast freezer. Bitter cold and absolute dark.

"Erin?" Zac said, and he felt her hand clench tight in his.

"No!" Erin cried.

Zac's eyes adjusted, and flat blankness came into focus. Korrie was gone. The room was gone. The entire hospital was gone. Night stretched out around them. He pulled Erin close to him. He could barely make out that they stood in an open field of cleared earth. The wind was so cold it stung his cheeks. A distant crane reached skyward in the moonlight, a red flasher blinking far above. An enormous earthmover sat parked in the dark where a mountain of soil rose in the stark night. "What the hell?" he said.

"It's happening again," Erin cried, "the interval."

"What?"

"This is what's been happening. It shifts."

"The light shifts?"

"Time!" Erin said. "This is 2022. Look at your phone."

Zac plucked his phone from his pocket and shook his head. "Can't be." He focused sharply: November 1, 2022. "This can't be!"

"We're in 2022," Erin said. "And Korrie is in 2021."

The sim bloomed in Zac's mind, the black gap opening in the aftermath of a wave.

"We have to get out of here." He took her arm. "How did you get out?"

"I didn't," she said. "It just changes."

"How did you get back to Korrie?" He couldn't think fast enough.

"I don't know how. Time kept shifting. I was in the past sometimes." She looked away toward the Flatirons, and his eyes followed her direction toward the desolate moon-whitened stretch of earth. "I found Aidon Clype. I set a fire," she said. "I got her back."

He tried to make his brain analyze the dimensions of space-time and what would happen if they were caught in a strand of time that was severed. Not the same strand as Korrie's.

Reason eluded him. "How has it been happening? Describe it."

"It flips, and it's a different time. It's been happening since around 9:30 this morning. It shifted to when Korrie was taken, and it went back and forth all day. Maybe once an hour or so. But not like this, not into the future."

"Oh no," Zac said.

"What?" Erin said.

"The waves." He shook his head. "How could you possibly be affected by the waves?"

"I don't know."

Zac thought for a moment. "My God," he said.

"What?" Erin looked into his eyes.

"In the sim, the waves end in destruction." He explained as fast as he could. "Things that have occurred are destroyed, and time splices shut." He took hold of her arm. "Did you lose any time?"

"Yes." Erin's eyes narrowed with concentration. "There was something missing. A piece I couldn't remember."

So it was happening. Mark's words returned to him. *The contents of the gap do not survive.*

"When was the last one?" He tried to steady her with his hand beneath her elbow. "How long did it last?" He had to know how close they were to the crowns of the two blast fronts.

"I'm not sure. They—"

Fluorescent light glowed oystery bright around them. Zac stood in the warmth, clutching Erin's elbow there in the confines of Korrie's hospital cubicle. They were back. Both of them rushed to Korrie's bedside. In perfect rest beneath the white sheet, in deep slumber, her chest rose and fell. Relief beyond understanding.

"Thank God," Erin said.

Zac checked the monitor, the green peaks pulsing in their neat, even row. Beeps soft and constant.

Erin took Zac's hand again and said, "Is it okay now?" She looked up at him. "Is it over?"

"I don't know," he said. "Maybe not."

Chapter Forty-Five

~

Erin sat on the edge of a sagging hospital chair at Korrie's bedside, exhausted and stunned into some sort of dazed tranquility. It was as if the events of the day had happened ages ago, and her memory of them seemed aqueous and impressionistic.

The pink had returned to Korrie's cheeks and lips, her chest rose and fell, and every so often her eyelids fluttered as if she were going to wake. The monitors on the other side of the gurney showed the steady measurements of her blood oxygen, her heartbeat, her respiration. All in perfect rhythm. The ER nurse had checked her reflexes, which were normal— a good sign.

Erin's injuries throbbed with thickening trumpets of pain as her initial dose of medication faded. And soon she would have to stand and head to the restroom, but for this moment, all she wanted was to stay like a sentry and watch Korrie sleep. Her hand, her small hand, was warm, there, wrapped in Erin's. It didn't matter that what they'd been through was irreconcilable.

Sirens whined outside, and Erin heard the whooping of helicopters in the distance. She wondered if the accelerated tempo of the hospital staff outside their cubicle was because of the fire. How could she ever explain herself? She'd set that blaze in summer to carry into a past winter so she could bring back her child, dead and buried, from the hands of her killer, back to the world of the living.

Erin could see only Zac's shoes as he walked back and forth beyond the hem of the curtain. He repeatedly treaded the linoleum, talking on his phone in the hallway outside the cubicle. She'd explained as much as she could about what had happened, and it had thrown him into a state of turmoil. His whispers carried farther as his tone became more urgent. When he came around the curtain, he looked terrible, his face marked with worry, his eyes intense and anxious. "I don't know what to do," he said.

"About what?" Erin reached out her good hand to him.

"When you lost time, do you have any idea how long it was? The time you couldn't remember?"

Erin shook her head. "I'm not sure." She thought back. "It would have to have been longer than it would take to start the fire. For me, the order of things was reversed, so I knew I'd started the fire, but I couldn't remember when."

Zac looked perplexed. "That's so much more than we thought."

"More what?" Erin said.

"We were thinking it was small moments, déjà vu–length moments."

"No," Erin said, "it was definitely much longer than that."

"I have to get back to the lab." He took her bandaged hand and held it, gently but without thought. "But I can't leave you two here."

"We have to stay here, Zac." She said it softly, seeing how upset he was. "Stay with us."

He nodded. His eyes moved with the labors of his thoughts. "But I have to let them know." He raked his hand back over his hair. "But I can't leave you."

"Just stay," Erin said, trying to calm him.

"I can't." He shook his head. "I have to find some way to leave a record in case the worst happens. But whatever I leave would also be lost."

"The worst?" she said, her anxiety returning.

"What we learned today. The sim. It could happen any moment."

"I don't understand, Zac," Erin said. "What do you mean by 'the worst'?"

"The waves," he said. "We had no idea what we were looking at."

Erin felt the sharp resurgence of all her fears. "Meaning what?"

"I still have no idea why you were singled out—why you crossed that border. It's not even possible." He let go of her hand. "But what we did discover is that gravitational waves obliterate pieces of time when they sweep past. The thing that I know now that no one else knows is that it's more than mere seconds that we lose. It might be a minute or an hour. You lost serious time."

"What are you saying? Be clear, Zac."

His eyes grew red. "The last wave is . . . The last wave will come at 9:32. It will be when two massive gravitational blast fronts break over the quantum collapse of a white hole. It's the thing that might never happen again. I don't know how much time an explosion like that will steal. If it was fifteen minutes, I wouldn't care. Even if it was an hour, I wouldn't mind. But what if it's more? What if it's days or months? We could lose this time and end up before now. Before you got her back."

"No!" Erin cried. "I can't go back to that!"

"The sim showed something about the depth of it. About us. Our consciousness. Whenever these waves strike, they steal time from us, and something about us . . ." He drew a fist to his chest. "Something in our consciousness affects how much we lose."

"Can you do anything?" Erin looked at the clock on the wall. It was only seconds until 9:32. She reached toward him, to hold on to him. "What can you do?"

"There's nothing to do," he said. "And we won't remember this."

PART V

Once Again

Like as the waves make towards the pebbled shore,
So do our minutes hasten toward their end;
Each changing place with that which goes before,
In sequent toil all forwards do contend.
—William Shakespeare, Sonnet 60

Chapter Forty-Six

❧

8:25 AM
Friday, February 7, 2020 | 371 Nysa Vale Road, Boulder,
Colorado

Erin charged down the stairs, struggling into her new dressy coat, with her purse, phone, and keys in her hand, torturous high heels clacking against the wooden treads. According to the weather app, the high would be thirty-nine and the snowstorm would last much of the day, but she couldn't show up to this interview in her old hiking boots.

In the kitchen, Zac's soft humming mixed with the sound of the kettle beginning to whistle. Erin approached him, drawn as always to the sensuous orbit of warmth that radiated from him. He stood near the counter with a mixing bowl wedged in the crook of his elbow and a wooden spoon in the other.

"Whatcha making, mister?" Erin said.

Zac looked up. "Yikes. Who's this strange woman in my kitchen?"

Erin smiled and looked down at her interview outfit. "Do I look strange?"

"You look like a stranger." He stirred the batter in the bowl. "A very strange stranger."

"Thanks." She half-rolled her eyes. "Is this why you came home early from your trip, so I could have the benefit of your style commentary?"

"That and my world-famous banana bread."

"Oh," Erin said. "Banana bread." It was one of the things he made as well as she did. She kissed him. "I hate to miss out." As she buttoned her coat, she said, "I have to go. I have to get Korrie to school, and I can't be late." She woke her phone to confirm the time.

"I'll keep it warm until you get back. I'll make ginger butter. We'll have tea."

"Perfect."

"What time do you think? I have that wrap-up call with Walter in Hingoli."

"I have no idea." She tapped the appointment in the calendar on her phone. "Ten? Ten-thirty?" It was hard enough to make herself go to the interview, feeling like a mannequin of someone else, but now with the storm outside and the prospect of warm banana bread and hot tea inside, it was even harder to rush out of the house. But it was Sledding Day at school, and she needed to drop off Korrie on her way.

"That'll work, I guess." Zac smiled.

She turned to go find Korrie, who stood near the front door, fortressed inside heaping layers of lavender outerwear. Hat, scarf, mittens, button-up sweater, thermal pants, parka; permission slip for Sledding Day poking out of her pocket. On her right foot, a furry white boot; on her left, a pink sock.

Erin stopped. "Where's your other boot, Squid?"

"I don't know." Korrie looked down at her sock.

"Go find it." Erin said. "We'll be late."

Korrie didn't move. "I already looked."

"Korrie." Erin deepened her tone. "We have to go. The roads are bad, and I can't be late. You have sledding, and I have my interview. Please go find your other boot. Right now."

Erin made an instant parental inventory of her daughter. She looked tired, Erin thought, hadn't wanted breakfast; she'd have to check on her later, after the interview. "Go find your boot. Please."

Korrie stayed planted in place. "I told you I already looked."

"I don't have time for this, Squid." Erin felt artificially upright inside her coat.

"But I'm having a hard morning."

"Well, so am I," Erin snapped back. She stopped. She called a halt to this frenetic drive, one that was not even her own. *This is not me,* she thought. She put down her purse. "Why is it a hard morning?"

"Because I feel weird."

"In what way, Squid?"

"Hot," Korrie said. "Melty and sleepy."

Erin knelt in front of her and laid her hand across her forehead. So warm. "That's because you have a fever, sweetheart." Erin took a closer look. Korrie's cheeks were flushed and her eyes were bloodshot and glistening. Something purled in Erin's head, something she couldn't quite grasp, as if it were submerged and drifting away in the current ahead. Something about time being so short. "Does anything hurt?"

Korrie shook her head. Her lips were dry, and Erin wanted to smooth some balm on them. She unzipped Korrie's coat and unwrapped her scarf. The manic pressure she'd felt about the interview began to dissipate and, with it, the desire to be that other person. Maybe she would just have to settle for being who she'd always been. "I'm sorry, sweetheart," she said, "but you're going to have to stay home today."

Tears filled Korrie's eyes. "It's Sledding Day."

"I know," Erin said. She slipped Korrie's coat and hat off. "But when you're all better, you and Daddy and I can go to Kinnikinic. We'll go sledding together and then we'll go to the Dushanbe Teahouse and have lunch, okay?"

"Okay." She sounded disappointed but resigned.

"Sound good?" Erin smoothed back her hair from her forehead.

"Yep." Korrie leaned into her arms.

Erin picked her up and felt the heat as she laid her head on her shoulder. She headed into the kitchen. "Zac," she said, "we have a sick girl here."

He put down the bowl and the spoon and came over to them. He pressed the backs of his fingers to Korrie's cheek. "Pretty hot," he said. "Want me to take her?"

"No," Erin said. "I'll get her into her pajamas and get her under the covers."

"What about your interview?"

"Let me make her comfortable." She turned and took Korrie upstairs to her room and sat her on her bed. Thrown in the jumble of covers was her pair of hand-sewn pajamas. "Back into your reindeer jammies, m'lady?"

Korrie nodded. "Yes, please."

Erin helped her undress and get into her pajamas, and once she was tucked beneath the covers, she got a thermometer from the bathroom and returned to take her temperature. "One oh one, Squid," she said. "Not too bad." She sat next to her and laid her palm across her forehead. "I'll get you some medicine and some juice, okay?"

Korrie nodded again.

Before Erin went back down to the kitchen, she ducked into her bedroom and stripped off her horrible plasticky interview clothes. She unknotted her hair and put on sweats and a T-shirt. Comfort clothes.

When she returned to the kitchen, Zac was filling a loaf pan with batter. He looked up at her and smiled. "There you are."

"Here I are," she echoed. She reached into the fridge to get Korrie a juice box.

He put down the bowl of batter. "So we're having a change of approach? Or just a change of wardrobe?"

"Both, I think." Would this disappoint him? Would he have less faith in her if she didn't do what they'd talked about? "Could you hand me the elderberry stuff?"

He reached into the cupboard above the toaster, retrieved a dropper bottle of syrup, and handed it to her. "I thought the die was cast," he said, and he slid the loaf pan into the hot oven.

"But time is flying so fast, Zac. And I don't want to spend another minute feeling like someone else's project. And I don't want to be gone all day. And I don't want to give up on myself."

"That's what this was going to be? Giving up?" He looked at her quizzically, with a half-smile.

"I want to figure out something else."

Then, from the doorway behind her, Korrie said, "Mommy?"

There she stood, cheeks pink, eyes glazy, in the pajamas Erin had made for her. She'd put her pink socks back on.

"What's up, Squid?" Erin crossed to her, knelt, and gave her the juice box.

"Can I stay down here with you guys?"

"Of course you can," Zac answered.

"Sure," Erin said, and she lifted her into her arms.

Stepping over the clutter in the living room, she aimed for the sofa and eased Korrie down with her head on the armrest. She sat next to her on the edge of the cushion and squeezed a dropperful of syrup between her lips.

"Now," she said, tucking a pillow under her head, "we can do a quick story, and then you can sleep while the medicine works, and when you wake up, we can have your daddy's banana bread, okay?" She covered her with a quilt.

Korrie nodded.

"You start," Erin said.

"Um." Korrie curled deeper under the quilt. "Once there was . . . an elf," she said.

"Who lived in the woods," Erin followed. The smell of batter baking started to fill the room. She felt conflicted: glad to be keeping Korrie home on this bitter day, relieved not to have to negotiate the minefield of the interview, but fearful about the future.

"And slept in a nest," Korrie said.

"In the white winter night." She patted Korrie's leg and said, "Hey, Squid, I think a fire would be nice."

Korrie nodded yes.

As Erin stood, a feeling illuminated within her, the sense that she had the strength to take on whatever might lie ahead of her. She couldn't know what the future was, but she knew she could rise to meet it. She began to look for one of the boxes of the new matches she'd ordered, the special ones with the Christmas picture of the three of them on the front.

Chapter Forty-Seven

⁓

9:00 AM
Friday, February 7, 2020 | Patrol of the University of Colorado campus

Tom Drake was in no way ready to be back. He'd paid five hundred dollars for his One-Day Test Out in Commerce City. In Block Three, he had used more than the required half speed and force to maintain physical control during the cuffing procedure. He'd lost points there, but he'd passed. He passed the driving test easily. He scored twenty-five of twenty-five on his firearms skills test, with twenty-four body shots and one head shot on the silhouette. The testing was on one of the days when his shakes were under control. If it had been on a different day, he might have failed all of it.

But today at least, he was back. Snow fell slowly from the pearl-gray cloud cover, and he just wanted to be a competent vessel on this pure white day.

The dispatcher called out his unit number. She said, "You've caught a couple of PNBs, Tom." Pulseless non-breathers. Hopefully something he could handle. She gave him the address and let him know he would join the coroner at the scene. Rebecca. Tom would be glad to see her. She was the new coroner now, and Tom hadn't run into her for several months. The two of them had gone out a couple of times back in the day, once for a casual lunch, once to The Bitter Bar, where they got sloshed on one Kiss the Sky after another. But nothing ever came of it, no matter how Tom wished it had.

When he arrived at the scene, the light seemed to brighten. There was another PD vehicle and the coroner's van in front of the residence. Tom checked himself in the rearview. *Okay, Tommy?* He stepped out of his vehicle, onto the icy street and drew a breath of cool, crisp air. He tromped through the snow drifts, up to the open front door, and into the residence.

He greeted the other cops, who seemed to be unconcerned and unhurried. In a tidy little back bedroom, he found Rebecca. She walked up to him, and it seemed like such a warm greeting when she said his name. "Drake."

"Beccs," he answered.

Her tech moved out of the room, peeling off his nitrile gloves.

"Not much to see," she said. "Come have a look."

On the bed, lying in what seemed like very deliberate positions, lay an elderly couple, fully dressed, side by side.

Rebecca held ID cards and pill bottles in her hands. "Would you like the details?" she said, with a smile.

"Sure." Tom took his notepad and pen from his pocket.

"The decedents are, respectively, eighty-eight and eighty-six. Our lady here," Rebecca nodded toward the body, "seems to have cleared out a month's prescriptions of zolpidem and hydromorphone." Tom looked at the old woman and wrote down his impressions. Delicate bone structure. Skin finely wrinkled and slightly spotted, with the beautiful translucency of being ancient. *Still lovely,* he thought. Though the lips were tinged blue, they were colored with traces of a shimmery pink lipstick that gave them a lavender cast, a certain ghostly loveliness.

"And this fine gentleman," Rebecca continued, "cleaned out his supplies of zolpidem and hydromorphone followed with a bit of a bourbon chaser. Quite a party." She pointed to a bottle on the dresser. The old man's head was slightly tilted toward the old woman.

Rebecca stepped closer to Tom, and as she typed on her tablet, he noticed her hands. Purple nitrile gloves, long fingers, no rings. "So what are you thinking?" he said.

"No injuries," she answered, "there are no signs of entry, nothing missing." Now two of her techs came in with body pouches and gurneys.

Tom stepped aside.

"Let's go out," Rebecca said, and for a second Tom's heart flopped happily in his chest. Then he realized she meant "outside." He followed her through the living room and out onto the front porch. She wrapped her arms around herself in the cold, and snowflakes drifted to her feet. He considered offering her his coat. Or was that too old-fashioned?

"We'll run their samples through Tox, but it looks to me like those two decided to proceed together to the nearest exit."

"Double suicide," Tom said.

"Yep."

Tom nodded. He thought about the two old people, how they'd gotten dressed up for each other. He wondered what someone would say on such an occasion. He thought about their last living moments together, how they had lain down, side by side, hands touching. The last romantic gesture of a couple of fine old fossils.

"So," Rebecca said, "I think that's it really." He loved her smile, the way it was slightly too wide for her face.

What if he said something now? He checked himself. He was only the smallest bit shaky. Besides, she would understand. She'd known cops her whole life. Certainly, he wasn't the first guy she knew with PTSD. "Hey," he said. "Beccs." He sounded more stern than he meant to.

"Drake," she said, pretending to be very serious.

He laughed. And he hadn't laughed for a long time. She laughed with him. "So," he continued, "I would like to give you a call sometime."

"Sure," she said, but now her techs were rolling the gurneys out of the house, bringing out the old couple to load into the van. Tom stepped back. "Call anytime," she said, and she followed the gurneys to the curb. He wasn't sure how she meant it now. And while he tried to figure it out, she got into the van, and she was gone. *Bravo Zulu, Tom,* he thought. *Well done.*

Chapter Forty-Eight

〰

9:32 AM
Friday, February 7, 2020 | 371 Nysa Vale Road

Erin lay on the sofa, Korrie curled asleep against her. She decided then that this was her new favorite stage of Korrie's childhood. She'd said that about every stage so far. Newborn, infant, baby, crawler, talker, walker, quizzer, entertainer. But this was really the best. Now they were really talking about things, creating together, thinking together. And Korrie was so smart. She and Erin played a game in which they built a story in turns, five words at a time, always beginning with, "once there was a" something. A monkey, a fairy, a flower. Early on, Korrie ended each tale with the protagonist successfully going potty, which she found hilarious. But by age six, the stories were filled with missions to save captured sisters or find undersea homelands.

Once there was a child, Erin thought. It was a little bit breathtaking to think that the universe had entrusted this small star into her care. She wanted wholeheartedly to do everything right, even when she couldn't be sure what it was.

Her cell phone hummed in her pocket, and she pulled it out. The caller ID read "Peregrine Elem."

"Shoot," Erin whispered as she connected with the call. She'd forgotten to phone the attendance line and notify the school that Korrie would be absent. "Hello?"

"Mrs. Fullarton?" The voice was familiar, slightly annoyed.

Erin pressed the phone tighter against her ear. "Yes."

"This is Jeanna," said the voice, "in the office at Peregrine Elementary."

"Right." Erin sat up halfway. "I meant to call. Sorry." She kept her voice low. "Korrie has a fever," she half-whispered, "and we're staying home today."

"Okay," Jeanna said, "thanks for letting us know," a little jab of sarcasm attached to each syllable, a backhanded comment Erin chose to dismiss.

After she'd disconnected from the school, Erin lay back into the sofa cushion, Korrie's head against her chest, and gazed into the fireplace. The fire she'd started was going out, dwindling embers dropping down into the ashes below. On the coffee table lay the matchbox with their Christmas picture printed on the front. If she wanted to keep the fire going, she would need to get more logs and kindling from the mudroom. But she didn't want to disturb Korrie, and so she decided to let her sleep as long as she needed to, even if the fire went out.

Chapter
Forty-Nine

❧

11:00 AM
Friday, February 7, 2020 | 64 Ebony Lane, Boulder, Colorado

Aidon Clype slammed the door of the trailer as he shambled out into the fucking cold. *Fucking freezing, god damn mother-fucker.* Under cover of the carport, he yanked open the door of his truck, climbed in, and started the engine. *Turn on some fucking heat.* He turned the blower up all the way and angled the vent toward his face. He was late. He'd overslept by two hours. Didn't have any clean clothes to wear. Didn't have time for cereal even.

The night before had been a total dud. Couldn't make himself feel better no matter how much he drank. No one to drink with. Just sitting there at The Old Grizz by himself, watching the TV because there was nothing else to do. Blew a chunk of cash. Couldn't skip out on his tab because of that fucking bartender. *Suspicious fuck.*

Snow flying everywhere. Everything white and buried. Miserable fucking bullshit. Expected him to get out there and freeze to death in the middle of fucking winter. For crap money. Not even enough to pay the rent to that whiney little dickhead of a roommate. And what was the point if he had nothing to look forward to? Not one tiny bit of pleasure in a long fucking time. How long had it been since the last one? Months. He turned on the defroster. And this shitshow of a storm. It was going to be a long, horrible day. And this was all there was now. Just one day after another, and not one god damn good thing ever. He was tired of it. He needed something to keep him going. He deserved at least one thing to get him through to the fucking weekend. Why not? There was nothing to stop him from having a moment of enjoyment out of this whole miserable crapfest. He could go out and find one. One pretty little thing to make him feel good.

He backed his truck out of the drive and dropped the plow onto the fresh snow. He was instantly all perked up. Much better now that he had a plan. *Hold up.* He stopped. From somewhere, a thought plinked into his head. *If you're going looking, remember your rifle. Better safe than sorry.* He had to remind himself of the stupidest things.

He parked again, got out of the truck, sniffed up a headful of this fucking frozen air. He ran for the trailer door and got inside. In the living room, there stood his crusty old roommate, that puny little fuck.

He said to Aidon, "You got the rent?"

"Fuck," Aidon said, "Are you on that again? I said I'd get it to you."

"That was a week ago." He pulled up the pathetic pajama bottoms that almost drooped off his ass.

Aidon headed toward his room. In the back of his closet was his uncle's M16. This was a tough-ass fucking weapon.

Dark and fucking ominous. Maybe even the actual one his uncle killed those motherfuckers with in Iraq. Aidon wished he could have been there. He'd gone online to learn how to handle a semiautomatic, and when he did a little target practice with it, he turned out not to be the greatest marksman yet, but the one bottle he did hit exploded like a fucking grenade. He grabbed the rifle and the only extra magazine he had. Quick as kaboom, he put them in a pillowcase and charged back out toward the front room.

His roommate was still pinned to the carpet in his floppy slippers, planted in the center of the room. The old man said, "I have to pay bills, you know."

"Yeah," Aidon said, "I'll get it as soon as I can." He blew through the front door.

"See that you do!" the old man called after him.

Piddly little fuck.

Chapter Fifty

❧

Tom sat alone in the warm airflow in this new Interceptor, waiting for the light to change at the corner of Twenty-sixth and Pearl. It was after 1:30. He wondered whether it would be a good idea to call Rebecca, what with the shape he was in.

Snowflakes descended on delicate white threads, micro-impacts of ice crystals against the windshield. When he glanced at his surroundings, he realized he was off his schedule and he'd forgotten to take a code seven. Ahead on Spruce Street was his old stomping ground, the natural grocery store, but also around the corner was Nate's favorite burger place. A pang of nostalgia struck him, a wish that he could return to the time when they were like blood brothers and Nate trusted him. He could pull into the drive-through and order some junk the way they used to on occasion. Or he could park in the lot of the natural store, haul his numb rear end out of the vehicle and go in and get something healthy. Salad and sesame sticks or something. He smiled at the memory of how they used to hassle each other about their diets. Nate's stomach-of-steel diet, he used to say, as opposed to Tom's fussy-sprout-eater diet. Tom decided to pull into the drive-through and procure a serving of junk, for memory's sake.

It was late enough that there was no line in the car lane. He pulled right up beside the speaker and ordered a burger and cheese fries. The guys would be proud. The teen-girl voice from within the speaker box gave him his total and instructed him to drive up to the window.

In front of him in the lane sat another vehicle, a black pickup, the customer driving it reaching out and paying for his food. Tom's ALPR picked up the plate and displayed the registered owner's name and address; not hotlisted, no warrants.

As he dug his wallet out of his pocket, he noticed there was a bumper sticker on the rear gate of the truck. He always liked to read bumper stickers—"Wag More, Bark Less," for example, "Property of the Denver Broncos," "Zombie Response Vehicle"—that kind of thing. When he'd nosed his vehicle up close enough to read the sticker on the black pickup, he leaned forward. "Honk if you want to suck my dick," it said. He went furious inside at the filth of it. His heart pounded at his ribs. Here was this foul little puke of a human being, spewing profanity everywhere he went, in front of decent people, families, children. The kind of person who lowered everyone into the sewer with him. Tom couldn't stand that kind of behavior.

The truck inched forward, away from the window, but before it could get to the curb, Tom hit his lights and gave a blast of siren to signal the driver. He knew no one gave tickets for obscenity anymore, but he could do it. It was still on the books. And this was really ticket-worthy. He gave a quick wave to the girl in the drive-up window and told her he'd be back. The brake lights on the truck reddened and then went dark. As he reached for his cite book, he got on his loudspeaker and instructed the driver to pull over.

The truck took off. "No way," Tom said. It turned onto the roadway and sped northbound.

He followed it and radioed in the call, letting a dispatcher know he was making a stop. "In pursuit," he called. "Twenty-sixth and Spruce." Somehow, his mind whirred smoothly into high-rev focus, a calm separateness from the discomfort tightening in the center of his chest as he pursued the truck.

The dispatcher came back: "Officer in pursuit, Twenty-sixth and Spruce." The voice of someone he knew well—Jackie, a longtime friend.

Tom accelerated to catch the truck. "Black Ram Niner Tree Six Henry David Queen," he called over the radio.

The truck ran a red, clipped an SUV in the snowy inter-section, and swerved north onto Twenty-eighth. Tom men-tally added hit-and-run to the offense of evasion and relayed it to Jackie. As he pursued the truck northbound through the storm, his engine crescendoed, the hum as frightening and thrilling as it was when he was younger.

Tom used his lapel unit. "Northbound Twenty-eighth approaching one-nineteen."

"Copy," Jackie replied.

Vehicles were slow to clear the snowbound route. The truck darted from lane to lane, putting distance between itself and Tom.

Tom pushed his vehicle faster. Discomfort. Nausea. Exhilaration.

The truck veered right. Took off onto the highway.

"Northbound one-nineteen."

"Copy."

Unit speed eighty-nine. Roads sanded but pretty damn perilous. Hard breathing. Heart rate. The white fields opened around him. Chest twinges. Vest tight. Gray trees like lace on the edge of the world.

He traced the black road north behind the truck. Chirps of the radio and the swing of the sirens. Tom called, "Proceeding northbound."

"Copy."

He raced along the highway between the soccer grounds and the reservoir. His past. The truck skidded on the road ahead and then righted itself and pulled into the left shoulder lane. Tom followed, feeling the vibration of the rumble strips under his tires. Unit speed ninety-four.

Time seemed to sponge up the space around him. What was he even doing out here? Did he think this was somehow valiant? He knew he'd never get his old life back, but didn't he still want to regain some sense of the man he'd been? Yet instead, he felt ridiculous. Like he was playing at being a cop, but really he was just nauseated and dizzy and scared of losing control of this vehicle. He followed the truck up the inner shoulder and passed the IBM plant and the shopping center. The highway passed over the ditch.

The truck took a sudden tack right across both lanes, and Tom thought for a moment that the driver might be giving it up, but instead he veered onto the shoulder.

Tom grabbed his lapel mic. "He's ditching at Eighty-third. He's ditching out."

The truck piled down the exit ramp and spun across the intersection onto the frontage road.

Tom slowed as his tires gabbled over the railroad tracks. The truck decelerated, no brake lights. It crawled down the edge of the thin gray road and slowed to a halt.

Tom stopped a safe distance behind him, flicked off his siren, and got on his speaker. "Get out of the vehicle," he called.

The truck sat immobilized at the road's edge. No movement from the driver.

He repeated, "Get out of the vehicle. Now!"

No response.

Tom opened his door, shielded himself behind it, and drew his weapon. He shouted, "Put both hands out the window. Now!"

Two hands appeared. From within the truck, the driver yelled, "I'm just out of gas."

"Open the door from the outside and get out of the truck!"

Hesitation.

Adrenaline. But then compliance. The door opened, and a man stepped out with his hands above his head.

Tom trained his weapon on the suspect and took two steps forward, yelling, "Step away from the vehicle." He recognized the man's face. It was the creeper from that day at the library. The one who'd slipped away. A wide slice of pain peeled open in the left side of Tom's chest. He staggered.

The suspect leaped toward his own vehicle.

Tom tried to capture a breath against the fierce pressure in his chest, tried to issue a command, but he could not.

The man pulled out a rifle, fired a drumroll at Tom. Hit him. Hard to say where. Vest. Pain drilling all around his chest and neck.

Tom returned fire. Body shot, head shot, body, body, body, body until the man dropped.

Tom reeled. Pain turning him inside out. He reached for his lapel unit. It hung in pieces against the front of his jacket. Shattered plastic. Wires wet with blood.

He staggered across the outstretched white terrain to where the suspect lay, and he kicked away the rifle. The man was dead. Head shot above the eye, no free bleeding.

Tom picked up the rifle and fought to get back to his vehicle. Sweating like a worked beast in the freezing air, he consciously instructed his legs: *Left, right. Left, right. Hurry up.* Equatorial fricking heat. A half ton of deadweight descended on his chest. Had to retreat and find some air. Deep breaths. Had to sit down. *Left, right, left, right. Time to puke, I think. Hurry now. Sit down.* He crumpled into his cruiser and got on the radio.

"Shots fired!" he shouted. "Shots fired! Officer down."

"Tom," Jackie called, "you're injured?" There was the echo of a cathedral in the coppery sound of her voice.

"I'm hit!" He felt the warmth of his blood seeping into his collar. "I'm hit, Jackie! And I might be having a heart attack."

"Okay, Tom," she came back. "It's okay—we're en route. You're running hot, grade one." Her end of the line chirped and crackled. "Tom!"

He forced a barely audible "Okay."

Other voices, other responses played on the radio. They knew where he was. He felt with trembling fingers around his ear. It didn't seem to be all there. Protruding from the side of his neck were fragments of shrapnel from his exploded lapel unit. A gash. Warm, fresh blood flow. He couldn't apply pressure because of the fragments. Knew he wasn't supposed to pull them out. Light and dark pulsed with his spasming heart. *Just sit here and try not to bleed to death. No dying today.*

It would be too absurd to die over a stupid obscenity ticket. Out here in the drifting white. If he were to die out here, it would be Rebecca who would come as coroner to claim him. Ironic. He'd always thought she was very enchanting. She would be a regret he would take away with him.

He started to feel a sweetness, the pressure of part of him squeezing himself out of the top of his head, rising upward. *No, no, no.* He fought with his mind to stuff himself back in. He heard a siren. *Thank God in Heaven, they're here.* But it wasn't a siren. It was music. Where was music coming from? He tried to sit up straighter. To listen for it. *Oh, come on,* he thought. *Exit music? Am I hallucinating my own exit music?* But no, it wasn't music either; it was the sound of crying. Someone was crying. He turned his throbbing head, trying to locate the origin. With both arms, he pulled himself out of his vehicle and stood swaying in the scatter of bright snow shards. The crying was coming from the direction of the suspect's truck. There he still was, primary piece of crap accounted for, his dead body lying pancake on the pavement.

He has someone in there.

The horizon tilted upward as Tom staggered toward the truck. He stepped over the body and looked through the open door into the cab. The crying came from some sort of bundle in the passenger footwell. The sound of a child. Tom moved his feet as if they were big puppet shoes attached by strings to his hands, and he edged around the hood to the other door. He pulled it open and saw movement within a canvas bag. Small. So small.

He knelt in the snow. "I'm a police officer," he said, "I'm going to get you out of this." The crying grew sharper. "It's okay now," he said, "you're safe," and he untied and opened the canvas bag. Glittery little-girl snow boots wriggled toward him. He widened the opening of the canvas bag and tugged it off her.

A little girl, six or seven. Terrified. Red teary eyes and wet nose. "Help me," she cried as she leapt against his chest. He braced himself with one arm and put the other around her. Then she drew back from the sight of him and said, "There's blood!"

"It's okay," he said, "help is coming." He blinked hard, trying to stay with her. "Did he hurt you?"

"He hit me," she wailed.

Sirens moaned in the sharp air. Finally. He held her against him and turned so he could sit down. "It's okay now," Tom told her. "We'll be okay now." Backup was almost here. He could hold on. He pulled in a breath so cold it made him cough. "What's your name?" he asked.

"Brennay," the child said. "It's Brennay."

"Okay, Brennay," he said. "I'm Tom."

Sirens screaming. Approaching. Several vehicles whining in chorus. Red and blue light streaking across the snow.

"We're okay now. Here they come."

The pure white world billowed before his eyes like waves on an ocean. Tires grinding into the snowy surface on the far side of the truck. Radio sounds. Lots of voices. More tires.

"Here!" Tom called over the sirens. "We're here!"

Chapter Fifty-One

≈

5:32 AM
Saturday, June 20, 2020 | 371 Nysa Vale Road

At sunrise on the summer solstice, Zac stepped softly out onto the front porch of the house and locked the door behind him. The cool, sweet, first-light scent emanated from the pines, and he inhaled deeply. Joyfully. He walked out onto the gravel path toward the garage, stopped, and looked back at the cottage. The upper windows reflected the lavender tinge of the early morning sky. Behind one window, Erin slept. Behind the other, Korrie. He'd looked in on them as he got ready to go. What was it, he wondered, that made his heart brim over like that, seeing the people he loved sleeping, lost in their dreams, serene?

He felt as if he were forgetting something. His tablet and his printouts were in his messenger bag. He patted his pockets. Wallet, key fob, phone. He didn't need anything else. He would get coffee on the way. It was a four-hour drive to Aspen, and then he would have breakfast with the group once he got to the Aspen Center for Physics. The presentation he'd prepared was informal, part of the summer conference, but he was nervous about it.

Loop quantum gravity was still seen as heresy by much of the old guard, and he wanted them to embrace this idea he was presenting, to join him in his perilous search. His mathematics showed that according to the laws of time-reversal symmetry, spacetime retained phantom memories of everything that had ever happened, even those fragments that appeared to be dismantled in the passage of gravitational waves. Traces of their existence could be found in the ultra-high-frequency memories left behind after the parent grav-wave memories could no longer be detected. Memories of memories. Orphans.

He would present his paper and do his best to reply to the barrage of skepticism he expected to follow. Then he would return home.

It was going to be his night to cook, and he wanted to make his farfalle pasta, butterfly wings in red sauce with spicy sausage. Korrie was big enough to help now. He would ask her to butter the garlic bread and put together the salads, and she would sing her little absent-minded tunes about elves and fairies and ladybugs while she worked. Erin would putter around the periphery the way she did whenever someone invaded her kitchen.

When dinner was ready, the three of them could sit together and talk about what had happened that day. He projected himself forward into that future to remind himself to gather that precious memory and hold it in the waves of his mind, his own quantum realm that rippled on and on in the endless history of time beyond time, because if the math was true, the universe recorded even the slightest electromagnetic pulse in time. And he wanted to keep every millisecond that was his.

Chapter Fifty-Two

◡

9:32 AM
June 20, 2020 | 371 Nysa Vale Road

Erin woke with an arm flopped over her eyes and a leg thrown across Zac's side of the bed. It took her a second to remember what day it was, the day of his presentation. He must have left hours ago, and he wouldn't be home until the end of the day. She hoped it would go well for him, but she wouldn't be surprised if he came home disappointed. He described his project to her as the quantum realm's metaphor for the way human memory was a longing for timelessness. She wondered if it would be too much poetry for minds made of math.

She mulled, as she started to wake, about all the things she could do today. Anything she wanted. She and Korrie could take a little hike and gather some wildflowers for the house. And then tonight, it would be Zac's night to cook, and they would have their butterfly pasta, always his first choice.

Her thoughts were interrupted by the sounds of guitar strumming. Zac had been teaching Korrie how to play

"Blackbird" on his old Martin acoustic. The words were indistinct, and she thought Korrie would probably make up her own anyway. She was her own little composer, her own small symphony, her own harmonica whenever she laughed. It was probably time to take her to the music shop and buy her a guitar for her little hands.

"Squid?" Erin called to the other room.

"Mommy?" *Thump, thump, thump.* Little bare feet on the hardwood planks. And then the soaring lavender flurry of Korrie taking a flying leap to their bed in her sequined tulle tutu.

"Argh," Erin groaned as Korrie landed on the comforter and rolled onto her stomach. Erin poked her ribs and stomach. Korrie giggled to the brink of hysteria. "What do you think you're doing?" Erin said, still poking. "Are you flying? Is that what you're up to?"

"Ah," Korrie sighed, calming a bit and brushing the hair from her face.

"What's our plan for today, m'lady?" Erin said.

Korrie put a finger up to her mouth. "I think . . . we should . . . um . . . build a skyscraper with an ice cream store at the very top."

"Or," Erin said, "we could go for a hike and pick some flowers so everything is beautiful when your daddy comes home."

"Well," Korrie said in her mock grown-up tone. "If you think we have enough time for such a thing."

"I think we're fine." Erin smiled. "We've got time."

Acknowledgments

My gratitude runs deep and wide. I'd like to start by expressing special admiration for Carlo Rovelli, from whose beautiful book *The Order of Time* I gleaned as much as I could about loop quantum gravity.

To the amazing Sandra Bond for her long hours of hard work, for her advice, her patience, and her persistence. To the fine people at Crooked Lane/Alcove who made it possible for this story to see the light of day—Ashley Di Dio, Jenny Chen, Madeline Rathle, Melissa Rechter, and Matt Martz—and to Jill Pellarin for such precision and expertise, and to Chelsey Emmelhainz for her keen editorial eye and sound counsel.

To the members of Salon Denver and to Kimberly McClintock and Phyllis Barber, thanks for listening to the earliest drafts. To my friends and colleagues at Lighthouse Writers Workshop, I'm immensely grateful for everything you've taught me, all you've shared, for your love and camaraderie, with special thanks to William Haywood Henderson, Mike Henry, and Andrea Dupree. To the writers who take my workshops, thank you for your trust and for bringing your creativity to the world. To Tiffany Quay Tyson and

Acknowledgments

Emily Sinclair for the days of SBD and to Shannon Skaife, Shari Caudron, Jay Kenney, and Greg Jalbert of The Supper Club. I'd also like to recognize Joy Roulier Sawyer for her kindness of spirit and Erika Krouse for not doing the fainting lesson in my honor. I also thank Karen Palmer, Alexandre Philippe, Amanda Rea, and Jenny Itell.

I send out into the deepest echoes of time my gratitude for having known Chris Ransick, for poetry and for song, for bourbon and wabi sabi, and for Grand Lake.

To my family, I thank you for your boundless love, for giving me endless courage, and for enduring my writing schedule. To Peter, for your help in the beginning; to Tim, for your inspiration; to Neill, for your encouragement; and to George, for your advice at the ending and for all and everything.